A PRAIRIE HOMICIDAL COMPANION

Also by Brian Landon:

Novels

A Grand Ol' Murder (Doyle Malloy #1)
The Case of the Unnecessary Sequel (Doyle Malloy #2)

Anthologies

Why Did Santa Leave a Body?: Yuletide Tales of Murder and Mayhem

A Prairie Homicidal Companion

To my hopefully non-homicidal reader. All the best to you!

A Doyle Malloy Mystery

Brian Landon

NORTH STAR PRESS OF ST. CLOUD, INC.
St. Cloud, Minnesota

First Edition: September 2012
Electronic Edition: September 2012

Printed in the United States of America

Published by
North Star Press of St. Cloud, Inc.
P.O. Box 451
St. Cloud, Minnesota 56302

www.northstarpress.com

www.northstarpress.com   Facebook - North Star Press

Dedicated to Claude and Tena Talbott,

long-time residents of the small town where much of this novel takes place.

Special Thanks to Garrison Keillor,

who continues to be strong, good-looking, and above-average.

PART I

July, 1986

Garrison, North Dakota

Three blocks east of the Walleye statue

1

His palms were sweaty. He hated that. It was bad enough that he was shaking. Not that he was nervous; surely his blood sugar was just a little off. But did it have to be so blasted hot? It made it far more difficult to hold the jar that held his namesake.

Bringing the jar to his chest, Fred Dillman wiped his brow with his free hand, then knocked on the front door of Edna Myrtle's house. He already knew she'd be home. He also knew she had several thousand dollars inside her house.

Dillman wasn't so naïve as to think old lady Myrtle would actually spend all her money on his pickles, even if they were homemade kosher dills made from only the finest pickling ingredients and the biggest, blemish-free cucumbers available at the McLean County farmer's market. Heck, Fred would be surprised if she bought one dang-blasted jar. Cheap old hag.

But he'd get her money. Just like he got all the others' money. Because he wasn't just the shy proprietor of the largely unsuccessful Dillman's brand.

Fred Dillman was the thieving serial killer the national press had begun calling the Friendly Companion.

He just wished these damned shakes would go away, along with his sweaty—

"Freddy? That's you, isn't it? Roger's boy?"

An affectionate grin spread across Dillman's face. "Yes, ma'am, it sure is. Though you can call me 'Pickles' if you want. Most folks do, being as I sell pickles 'n' all."

Edna Myrtle laughed in that sickly sweet fashion that annoyed Dillman to his core. His nickname, combined with his surname and his profession—it was all just too much. Everyone laughed. They couldn't help it. Everyone laughed at *him*. But that was okay. He embraced it. He wanted to be angry and annoyed. It made things easier . . . later.

"That's cute, dear," said Edna, regaining composure after a laugh that was a bit too hardy for a Catholic in these parts.

"Now, I don't want to give any wrong impressions, Ms. Myrtle. But I'm here to sell my family's famous Kosher Dills," said Dillman, proudly displaying the jar.

"I've got no money," said Edna abruptly. Then, perhaps backtracking as to not sound impolite, she said, "It's been a difficult few years since Walter passed away. And the bank hasn't been treating me too kindly."

"Oh, I understand, ma'am," said Dillman, not losing his grin. "Folks all over are feeling the same crunch. And speaking of crunch," he said, twisting off the lid of the pickle jar, "I'd be most pleased if you at least tried a free sample."

"That's a price I might be able to handle. But my momma always taught me that nothin's free."

"Tell you what," said Dillman. "Allow me to step out of this heat for a minute or two, and I'll consider it a fair trade."

Edna Myrtle smiled. "Well, all right then."

Dillman wiped a sweaty palm on the side of his pants as he slid past Edna Myrtle into her home that reeked of that nauseating musk of old people. He sniffed his pickles to clear his senses.

"I see you like your product," said Edna. "I take that as a good sign."

Dillman felt something wet on the front of his pants, and realized his hand was shaking so much that a sizeable splash of pickle juice had found its way out of the jar.

"Oh, shoot," said Dillman.

"Did you have yourself an accident, son?" asked Edna, looking down at Dillman's soaked trousers.

"No. Well, yes. But I didn't pee—"

"My, you're shakey," said Edna. "Do you have the diabetes? Walter did. Boy, that can be terrible if you don't keep a close eye on it."

"Yes, ma'am. Sometimes my blood sugar gets a little low. But don't worry about me. Would you like to try a pickle?"

"Just you wait a minute while I get you a glass of lemonade," said Edna. "That should help."

"That'd be just fine. Thanks, ma'am. Say, you don't happen to have a bathroom I could use, do you?"

"Just down the hall, dear."

Fred Dillman was hopeful that the preceding incidents may have been a blessing in disguise. If he had enough time to search her house for the money, then he might not have to kill her. Not that he cared whether she lived or died. But the whole process was rather distasteful. The body hitting the floor. Foaming at the mouth. Partially masticated portions of his family's award-winning pickles strewn about the linoleum floor. Then he had to clean everything, inside and out. And as a finishing touch, he always placed the jar of pickles in the pantry, as if they'd been there all along.

Who was he kidding. Of course he'd kill her. The Friendly Companion was becoming more famous than Dillman's Kosher Dills.

Dillman passed the living room when he stopped dead in his tracks. Lady Luck was definitely on his side today.

"Did you find the bathroom?" he heard Edna yell from the kitchen.

"Yes, ma'am," Dillman hollered back, though his eyes were fixed on what appeared to be an oversized ottoman at the foot of the recliner. It was wrapped in a bed sheet. As odd as it was, it also wasn't the first time Dillman had seen something like this.

Dillman got down on his knees and reached out a shaking hand toward the obtuse piece of furniture, then pulled his hand back when he realized his perspiration would soak the sheet. He wiped his hands on his pants the best he could, then turned around to make sure the old woman wasn't anywhere in sight.

He clenched his right fist and knocked on the rectangle. Dillman heard exactly what he was expecting—a hollow, metallic *clunk clunk*. Excited, he tore the bed sheet away, revealing a safe. It was a Patriot model; he could tell from the gold emblem in the middle. A 1940s unit? Dillman wasn't positive, nor did he care. As long as he could get into it. And if he couldn't, well, he knew someone who—

Crack! Pain exploded in the back of Dillman's head, sharp at first, then spreading. He reached for the pain, trying to find its source, but he could feel nothing but wetness. He turned his head, not sure what he was expecting to see, but definitely not expecting Edna Myrtle. She looked angry. Or was she sad? Did she know what happened to him?

Then he saw the rolling pin in her hand, but that didn't quite make sense, did it? It appeared to be leaking something all over the floor. Something red.

Oh. Just as the realization dawned on him, the rolling pin came down on his skull again, and the lights went out.

* * *

Dillman awoke to a loud knocking that split his skull. He opened his eyes to see three pictures swirling. He tried to rub his eyes, but discovered quickly that his hands wouldn't move. His shoulders worked okay. Did the old hag break his hands? He closed his eyes, then reopened them. Everything came into focus, just as the door burst open, unleashing a half dozen uniformed men. Were there really that many, or were his eyes playing tricks on him? When they descended on him and lifted him to his feet, he knew they were really there. What the hell was on his wrists? It was a tattered, brown leather belt. Probably belonged to the hag's dead husband. A belt around his ankles, too. Christ, she really did a number on him.

The police pulled him out the front door. When he looked behind him, the last thing he saw before he lost consciousness was the old woman, *that bitch*, handing his jar of pickles to the authorities.

PART II

September, 2012

Saint Paul, Minnesota

"You never know what's coming for you."
- F. Scott Fitzgerald

2

I don't get it," whispered Detective Doyle Malloy into Amanda Hutchin's ear as he looked around the crowd of smiling and laughing faces. Everyone was clapping. One elderly lady towards the back was dancing in the aisle to the tune of Norwegian folk music. "Why are we watching a radio show?"

The Fitzgerald Theatre, or the Fitz as the locals called it, was filled to the brim with fans of Garrison Keillor's long-running program.

"It's a chance to be a part of something special," said Amanda, wearing a modest blue dress instead of the usual suit she wore as a detective for the Saint Paul Police Department. "I used to listen to this show every weekend with my dad."

"Even the commercials are fake," said Doyle. "It doesn't make sense. How do they earn any revenue from fictitious powdermilk biscuits?"

"It's nostalgic," said Amanda. "C'mon, with our jobs, isn't it comforting to be whisked away to a more innocent time and place?"

Doyle had dealt with more murders in the past year as a private detective than in his entire career as a cop. His final case with a badge had been a high profile one involving a murder on Grand Avenue, which he'd barely survived with his head in one piece. But it'd given him enough clout that he presumed he could successfully make it as a private detective, along with his partner, William Wright. Unlike Doyle, William actually seemed to know what he was doing. Doyle preferred winging it.

However, Doyle quickly realized that life as a private detective was much more perilous without law enforcement behind him. During an adventure in Brainerd, Doyle and his crew had been stabbed, drugged, shot at, and kicked in the nuggets, all for a minimal paycheck. Since then, he'd been hesitant about taking any case without thorough background research, for which he usually relied upon William and Amanda.

"All this nostalgic innocence makes me wonder when the first body's going to hit the floor," said Doyle.

"No offense, but you're kind of ruining the experience."

"Sorry," said Doyle. "I'm going to get a cocktail. Want anything?"

Amanda shook her head.

Doyle stood up at the end of a song, and walked out of the auditorium and into the lobby during what sounded like was the start of a rather lengthy monologue. He probably would have enjoyed it more had he studiously sat in his assigned seat, but patience was never Doyle's strong suit.

He approached the well-dressed man bartending the quaint bar stocked full of presumably over-priced drinks.

"What can I get for you?"

"The usual," said Doyle.

The bartender surveyed Doyle for moment. "Do I know you?"

"It depends. Have you ever hired a private detective to investigate the murder of someone close to you?"

The bartender looked worried. "No."

"Then I guess you don't know me."

Scratching his head, the bartender said, "Can I get you a Budweiser or something?"

"No," said Doyle, taking out a business card. "Blueberry daiquiri. That's the usual. Next time I'm here, I want you to hand me a blueberry daiquiri, no questions asked."

"If you insist," said the bartender.

"And here's my business card. If anyone you know ever has trouble, have them give me a call."

"You got it."

After picking up his drink, Doyle, who was never skilled at finance, slapped a twenty on the table and told the bartender to keep the change. He considered it a business investment.

On his way back to his seat, Doyle accidentally bumped into a man with a long gray beard and a cowboy hat. A small amount of blue liquid splashed onto the man's white dress shirt.

"Oh, I'm sorry," said Doyle. "Please, let me help you get that out."

"No, son. Ain't no need to bother. There ain't no helping me."

"But I'm—"

"Just don't."

With a small shove, the man in the cowboy hat pushed Doyle aside and continued towards the bar.

Not knowing what to do, and feeling somewhat ashamed, Doyle proceeded back to his seat. It wouldn't be until later that evening that Doyle would fully understand the significance of that encounter.

3

nlucky Larry looked down at his blue-splotched shirt. "Shit," he muttered to himself. He actually felt bad about brushing off the young fellow who'd spilled his drink on him, but he wanted a glass of whiskey so bad, he really didn't care about much else. It'd been a hell of a week, and based on the phone calls he'd recently received, he may not have many weeks left.

"Can I get you some water?" asked the bartender.

"Shit, no. Make it a whiskey on the rocks."

"I meant for your shirt."

"I don't care about the shirt."

The bartender poured a whiskey on the rocks. Before handing it over, the bartender asked, "Is everything okay, Larry?"

Larry squinted his eyes. He didn't recognize the bartender, although that didn't mean the bartender didn't know him. After all, most people did know him, as long as they were familiar with Garrison Keillor's show. Unlucky Larry was the star of a recurring comedy bit in which everything that could go wrong for him did go wrong. He got tons of laughs every night. Although he hadn't laughed himself since the call from his daughter last Monday.

"More bad luck," he'd said to himself with a sad chuckle after the call.

Unlucky Larry wasn't just a stage name; in fact, he'd been known as Unlucky Larry since childhood when he was the only Norwegian adopted into a large Irish-Catholic family. That he didn't have the luck of the Irish didn't stop him from being the first in his family to graduate from college as a communications major and eventually getting into show business. Quite a leap for a kid growing up in the small town of Garrison, North Dakota.

But that was a long time ago, and his own kids had all grown up and were having kids of their own. Out of three daughters, only one of them, Clara, had left the state with a husband to make a life for herself. Another daughter, Tabitha, had also married, but only moved a few miles away to the "big city"—Minot, North Dakota. His other daughter, Mae, remained unmarried and stayed in Garrison where she'd grown up.

It was Tabitha who called him up from Minot to tell him about the murders. Not the brutal killings from twenty-some years ago, but brand new ones. Murders that sounded like the work of the guy they'd already put in prison. The guy who'd killed Unlucky Larry's wife Tess.

"It gets worse," she'd told him. "An article was published in the *McLean County Independent* this morning. It said you were in critical condition and were not expected to live through the week."

"I'm just fine."

"I know that. I tried calling you several times this morning, and when I couldn't get ahold of you, I called the guy who wrote the article. He had no idea what I was talking about."

"Who wrote it?"

"Lawrence Stiles, of Minot. Only he claims he didn't write the article, that it just showed up in the paper. Something's going on here, Dad. You better be careful. It sounds like someone has it in for you."

Not expected to live through the week.

Unlucky Larry took a drink of his whiskey on the rocks.

"Are you sure you're going to be okay?" asked the bartender.

"Not unless you know a really good detective," said Larry. "Or a bodyguard who can protect my aging ass."

The bartender shook his head. Then, a thought seemed to pop into his head.

"You know, I think I know someone who might be able to help."

Reaching behind him, the bartender accidentally knocked over a bottle of blueberry juice, which he'd just used to pour a drink. The juice spilled all over the table, drenching the business card he'd been reaching for.

"Shoot," said the bartender, shaking the business card. "Wouldn't you know it, the type was in blue ink, too."

Unlucky Larry rubbed his temples.

"Gee, I guess you sure live up to your nickname, don't you Larry?" quipped the bartender.

"Yeah," said Larry. "I sure do."

ll better?" asked Amanda.

"Much," said Doyle, taking a sip of the cold, delicious beverage in his hand. "What did I miss?"

"Keillor did one of his Guy Noir stories. Those are always so fun."

"You've lost me," said Doyle.

Amanda patted his knee. "Just relax. Enjoy your drink."

Doyle did as he was told. Even though he rarely went to a show that didn't include at least one power ballad—he never missed when Styx came to the Minnesota State Fair—he was content that he was spending time with Amanda. Their relationship had progressed substantially in the past year, not only in that she had moved into his small apartment in north Saint Paul, but they had also grown shockingly and unexpectedly comfortable with each other.

"And now ladies and gentlemen," announced Garrison Keillor into the vintage-style microphone. "I'm happy to present to you the unfortunate adventures of Unlucky Larry."

The audience applauded.

"Is this good?" asked Doyle.

"It's funny," said Amanda. "It's a recurring sketch, a comedy bit. You'll like it."

Doyle nodded. Then he was surprised to see the man he'd bumped into just moments earlier walk onto stage, sans the white dress shirt. At first Doyle thought the blueberry daiquiri had left such a stain that the man, Unlucky Larry apparently, couldn't wear it onstage. But the fact that Unlucky Larry was wearing a robe and a nightcap suggested this particular sketch didn't really require a dress shirt.

Unlucky Larry rubbed his eyes, stretched out his arms into the air, and let out a mighty yawn. "I think I'll make myself some coffee," said Unlucky Larry. Several loud bangs erupted, decorating Larry's robe in ribbons of red. He fell to the ground with a lifeless thud.

"That was a quick sketch," whispered Doyle to Amanda. "Are they normally this short?"

"I don't think—"

"I can see where his name comes from," continued Doyle. "I definitely didn't see that coming."

"That's not part of the show," said Amanda.

The audience was silent. No one coughed. The only sound was Doyle slurping as his straw reached the bottom of his glass. Then the audience, who was likely hoping they were part of some elaborate joke, began to panic. A woman behind Doyle shrieked. The aisles flooded with people trying to flee the auditorium.

"I'll call it in. You call William," said Amanda.

"I was thinking the same thing," said Doyle, although Amanda was already talking on her cell phone. Doyle pulled out his, too, and began dialing as he scanned the auditorium, searching for anyone who looked suspicious. With such a huge, scrambling crowd, it was impossible to see anything.

"William? William, is that you? I can barely hear you—it's really loud in here." Doyle held the phone to his ear as he swam against the tide of oncoming frightened theater patrons. He approached the bloodied body of Unlucky Larry. A few gawkers were nearby, but kept their distance from the body.

Doyle only heard a few words come through the phone. *What . . . bloody hell . . . yelling for?*

William, just like Doyle, was formerly a detective for the police. Unlike Doyle, he was from Scotland Yard, and also a rather good investigator. He'd lost his job due to a few minor issues with alcohol, his ex-wife, and working tirelessly on tracking down serial killers. William moved to the United States a few years back to stalk his ex-wife, but did some freelance detective work on the side. Doyle hired him to assist with what ended up being Doyle's final investigation with a badge. Since then, they'd been private detectives. Partners.

"William, I can't hear you. I think we have a case. Look up anyone who has association with a man named Unlucky Larry. He's a performer who lives up to his name. We'll need to move fast on this one."

Doyle looked down at his phone and saw it had disconnected. He really hoped he'd gotten through to William.

Amanda grabbed Doyle's shoulder. "Steven's on his way, but I don't think it matters. Reiser's going to put McNulty and Jenkins on this. They're next up in the rotation."

"Shit," said Doyle. "We need you on this one."

"Doesn't matter. Even if I was I was next up, Reiser doesn't know me or trust me well enough to put me on such a high-profile case yet."

Amanda had just been promoted from officer to detective first rank the year before, shortly after being transferred from Minneapolis to Saint Paul along with most of her colleagues. After the former chief of the MPD was caught breaking numerous laws to protect his homicidal son, the powers-that-be decided to clean house. Although she enjoyed working in Saint Paul, she was still garnering acceptance from her fellow detectives and from her new boss, Chief Cynthia Reiser.

"Let's just do what we can," said Amanda. "Things could change."

"How soon will Steven be here?" asked Doyle. Detective Steven Kanter had just been partnered with Amanda, and they'd been working through how their partnership would work. Steven seemed uncomfortable with Doyle's presence, even though Doyle tried to keep his interference in Amanda's work day to a minimum. "Does he know I'm here?"

"I'm sure he assumes it. Don't worry, it'll be fine."

"He loathes me," said Doyle. "I think he wants me out of the way so he can have you all to himself."

"I'm pretty sure that's not it. Besides, now's not really the time, Doyle. We'll talk about it later."

"Okay, but I'm not giving you up without a fight. I'll take him down."

"I know you will, my big tough guy. Now, let's secure the scene. Obviously the gunfire came from somewhere in the audience, so someone must have seen the shooter. Unfortunately, almost everyone cleared out right away, so we'll need to interview the few stragglers and hope that others will come forward after things have settled down."

"All right, that seems like a fine—"

"Waste of time!" said a familiar, exceedingly unpleasant voice from behind Doyle, near the side entrance.

"McNulty," said Doyle. "You got here in a hurry. Were you running a prostitution sting at the Kelly Inn?"

"That's how he met his wife, isn't it?" said Amanda, despite the fact she'd be spending far more time around McNulty than Doyle had to. She was only subjecting herself to further vexation from the gruff, boorish cop.

McNulty's face showed just a flash of anger, which quickly subsided. He smiled. "As a matter of fact," he said, "I was in the right place at the right time. Jenkins and I were having a stack of pancakes at Mickey's Diner when we got the call. We were closest, so I came running. Jenkins is bringing the car around as we speak."

"Good for you, McNulty," said Doyle.

"But seriously, Malloy, what are you doing here? You still a private dick? I find it hard to believe that someone with half a brain would actually hire a worthless son of a—"

"Can it, McNulty," said Doyle. "I was simply enjoying the show when the shots rang out and Unlucky Larry was turned into swiss cheese."

McNulty turned to Amanda. "And Detective Hutchins, I'm sure you're well aware that me and Jenkins are next up in the rotation. I really appreciate you two playing cops until we got here, but we can take care of the rest."

"Okay," said Amanda. "You have an awful lot of people to interview. The theater was sold out. Have fun with all of that."

"Don't worry, we'll work it out," said McNulty. "Tell you what. Since we'll be so busy, maybe I'll talk to Razor and see if she'll let you help us out by doing the next-of-kin notifications. Those always go better coming from a woman."

Razor was the name Amanda had been using for her boss, Chief Cynthia Reiser. This was the first time Doyle noticed that people beyond Amanda also referred to her as Razor. He'd never met her, but if names were any indication, Chief Reiser was probably not a very friendly person.

Despite McNulty's comment, Doyle could see Amanda bite her lip to refrain from saying something she'd later regret. Instead, he was surprised to hear her agree.

"No need to ask her, McNulty. I'll do it. Just make sure when I'm next up in the rotation, you don't try to usurp my authority."

McNulty curled his lip. "Whatever you say . . . *Detective.*"

Amanda tugged at Doyle's arm. "Let's go."

Doyle hustled after her. "Did you notice how he added some really unnecessary emphasis on that last word? That was downright sarcastic."

"Trust me, I'm used to it."

They stepped through the side exit and headed towards the parking lot across the street. "And please tell me why you offered to do the dirty work?" asked Doyle.

"The next-of-kin notification? You might want to get used to those."

"I did plenty of those when I was with the MPD."

"But you worked on celebrity cases, and when I met you, I can honestly say you didn't work too hard on them. Did you actually go out to deliver the bad news yourself?"

"Couple times," said Doyle. "I may have assigned those duties to a lower-ranking officer once in a while. Wait, wait, wait . . . so tell me again why we're doing this now? I understand you're fairly new to the position, but I'm sure you're familiar with the motto 'Volunteering Doesn't Pay.' So what gives?"

Amanda opened the passenger door to her Honda Accord and Doyle got inside. It was a role reversal that Doyle easily acclimated to. Amanda liked to wear the pants, and if anyone ever asked, Doyle admitted to being totally progressive, stereotypes be damned.

"I've been doing some long-term planning," said Amanda.

"Okay . . ."

"And since I live with you now, I'd like you to actually make a decent salary."

"The private detective business has been a bit slow, I suppose . . ."

"So here's what I've been thinking. When someone dies, who's most likely to hire you? The family of the victim, right?"

Doyle nodded.

"Especially when—" Amanda began.

"The two detectives in charge are complete buffoons like McNulty and Jenkins," said Doyle. "Brilliant!"

"And just to stoke the coals a little bit, I've been encouraging McNulty and Jenkins to give their own press conferences. You know— get them out there in the public eye."

"My God, Ms. Hutchins—you're downright devious!"

"Not devious. Just smarter than the idiots I work with," said Amanda.

"I can't believe Razor is okay with the gruesome twosome being the face of the SPPD."

"She doesn't know them well enough yet, so their public speaking opportunities might be short lived. "

"Nice," said Doyle.

"Meanwhile, whenever I'm assigned to a case, of course I'll solve it with flying colors."

"You could have been a criminal mastermind."

"Maybe, but I don't look so hot in orange," said Amanda with a wink.

"So what now? Head back to the batcave?"

Amanda nodded. "Call William, ask him to meet us there. Depending on the size of the family, we may have multiple homes to hit tonight. Let's get you hired. Then let's solve the murder before tweedledee and tweedledumb."

Doyle just shook his head in disbelief. "Amazing woman," he muttered to himself.

5

Amanda pulled the Honda into the parking lot of Doyle and William's headquarters, a poorly renovated dentist office on Central Avenue just north of Minneapolis. Here Doyle had met William a couple years ago when Doyle was in serious need of assistance cracking a case, and the only way he could do it was by hiring a private detective. The sad irony that he was a detective hiring another detective was not lost on Doyle, which was why he kept it on the down-low until Doyle and William formed an equal partnership.

The dentist office was in much better shape than years prior when William had been working and living there by himself. Doyle and William had received a fairly substantial check from actor Timothy Chapman as a reward for bringing the murderer of his maid to justice, and they used some of the proceeds to renovate the dentist office. They removed some rusty, abandoned dentistry equipment, painted the walls and the exterior, put down some new carpet. They even covered up the old "Reginald Jackson, D.D.S." sign with a brand new one:

MALLOY AND WRIGHT
DETECTIVES FOR HIRE
DAY OR NIGHT

"I hope William has some pants on," said Doyle. "I know he's a night owl, but sometimes he gets a little too comfortable in the office."

"Well, he does live here," said Amanda. "Maybe after a few successful investigations, he can move out of the file room and into an apartment of some sort?"

"Maybe," said Doyle. "Are you going to call up your new partner?"

"Steven? I will, once we have a solid plan. He'll be upset if I don't ask him to join us. Even if it is just the next of kin. He wants to be involved."

Doyle nodded. "He's not going to want me around. I'm telling you, he hates my guts."

"Settle down," said Amanda.

Doyle tested the doorknob to see if it was unlocked, which it was, and pushed the door open just a crack. "William—you got pants on?"

He was greeted by an all-too-familiar English accent. "Good Lord, Doyle—that happened once, and I already explained that I was merely trying to locate an important piece of evidence that I'd accidentally dropped down my trousers."

"I didn't believe it then, and I don't believe it now," said Doyle, pushing the door open. "Get some good shuteye?" Doyle looked at his watch. It was just after ten o'clock in the evening.

"Absolutely," said William. "Good thing, the way it sounds. We have a case?"

"Well, almost," said Doyle.

"I'm technically not assigned to this one," said Amanda. "But I did volunteer next-of-kin duties. So hopefully . . ."

"You'll get us the job. My goodness, you're a devious bird, aren't you?"

"That's what I said," said Doyle.

William pulled out a chair from behind the receptionist desk and sat down. He motioned for Doyle and Amanda to sit in the waiting room chairs closest to him. William pulled out a notebook.

"Very well," said William. "What have we got?"

Doyle motioned for Amanda to proceed.

"Larry Sanderson, known to fans of a *Prairie Home Companion* as 'Unlucky Larry.' He was shot on stage at the Fitz by someone in the audience. Hard to tell at this point what part of the auditorium the shots came from. The place cleared out fast. He was shot several times, so we have to entertain the possibility of multiple gunmen. We'll know more when ballistic information comes back."

William nodded. "On more of an anecdotal level, what do you know about this Sanderson fellow? He's an entertainer, yes? Any gossip from the tabloids? Was he going through a divorce, or did he lose all his money in the recession? Was he involved in anything scandalous? Do people keep up with him, like these Snookies and Kardashians and so on?"

"He wasn't that sort of entertainer," said Amanda. "He was a voice on a radio show, although he performed on stage to an audience when the radio show was being broadcast. The show is broadcast nationally, but it's a different audience than *Jersey Shore*."

"Very different," said Doyle. "There were many people on stage, but not a single tan line to be seen."

"What else do we know about him?" asked William.

"Well," said Doyle. "I . . . uh, sort of ran into him. Before he was shot."

"You did?" asked Amanda. "You didn't mention that."

"I was getting around to it. I accidentally bumped into him and got a little bit of my drink on his shirt. But it's okay—he didn't need it on stage. He changed into a pajama costume."

"That's not a big deal," said Amanda. "It shouldn't hamper our investigation at all. Why are you so concerned?"

"Because, the last thing he experienced on this earth was me annoying him. Now he'll be thinking about that for the rest of eternity. That's a heavy burden on yours truly."

"I think he'll get over it," said Amanda. "Besides, if you find out who shot him, I bet that'll go a long way. He might even forget the whole thing."

"Probably not. Centuries from now, he'll still be thinking about having a drink spilled on him, then getting shot and killed. That's a really bad day. You don't forget days like that."

"What the bloody hell are you two babbling about? Let's get to work," said William. "Do we know who the next of kin are?"

Amanda and Doyle shook their heads.

"Well, I'll find out," said William.

"How?" asked Doyle.

"Like I always do," said William. "Google. And failing that, his Facebook page, if he has one."

"Sounds like a start," said Amanda.

"How long before we have some info?" asked Doyle.

"Give me ten minutes," said William. "Then we can head out, convince the family that we're the best equipped detectives to handle this investigation, and then solve it."

"You make it sound so simple," said Doyle.

"Oh, it won't be. I'm certain of that. But we'll try to convince the family otherwise. And who knows—we may get lucky."

"Unlike Larry," said Doyle.

William smirked.

"Too easy?" asked Doyle. He didn't wait for an answer. "Too easy. I'll avoid those jokes from now on."

"No, you won't," said Amanda.

ere we go," said William, holding up some papers he'd just grabbed from the printer. "Larry Sanderson's living relatives."

"Do they live in the Cities here?" asked Doyle.

"One of his relatives, yes," said William. "A daughter, Clara Belmont, lives in Golden Valley."

"We can get to her real fast," said Doyle. "Any other kids?"

"Two other daughters," said William. "Tabitha Nichols lives in Minot, North Dakota, and Mae Sanderson lives in Garrison, North Dakota."

Doyle's ears perked up. "Garrison? That's where my dad grew up. He had his first job as a police officer there."

"Isn't that a pretty small town?" asked Amanda.

"Oh, yes . . . very small. More tumbleweeds than people."

"What about a spouse, William? Was there a wife?" asked Amanda.

William looked at both of them with a smile just ready to burst across his face. He looked like a little kid who couldn't hold back a secret.

"There was a wife, as a matter of fact," said William, looking at the print outs.

"Was? As in, either divorced or dead?" asked Amanda.

"The latter, unfortunately," said William. He didn't say anything else.

"You're holding something back, William—what is it? You're starting to make me nervous," said Doyle. "Out with it!"

"His wife, Tess Sanderson, was murdered in 1985. In Garrison, North Dakota."

Doyle was stunned. Before he had a chance to respond, Amanda asked, "Did they apprehend the killer?"

"They did," said William. He turned to Doyle. "Or rather, Officer Harold Malloy did."

Doyle could see it was now Amanda's turn to be stunned.

"It was his first big case," said Doyle. "My dad—he told me a lot about it when I was in my teenage years, when I was old enough to hear about his very first serial killer."

"Serial?" Amanda asked. She paled.

Doyle nodded. "It's what got him hooked. He was a cop for life after that. He was also the town hero. I just . . . don't understand how this is connected."

William sat back in his seat and made himself comfortable. "You have to realize that there may be no connection. Just because Larry Sanderson's wife was murdered twenty-some years ago doesn't mean that his own murder is related. It could be purely a coincidence."

"You've been a detective a long time, William. Do you believe in coincidences?" asked Doyle.

"No, not terribly. If there's a coincidence, there is usually a thread that ties the two things together. I was just saying it's possible they're not related," said William.

"The killer," said Doyle. "That my dad arrested. Where is he? Still in prison?"

"That, I think, will take a little more research," said William.

Doyle felt anxious. He didn't want to wait any longer. Amanda must have picked up on this, because she put a hand on his knee and said, "Why don't you stay here with William and get some more information. I'll call up Steven and we'll visit Clara in Golden Valley. We'll make sure we get you hired."

"That sounds good," said Doyle, but truth was, he was still nervous. Could there be a connection? Is the same killer on the loose, killing the surviving spouses of his former victims? It seemed unlikely, but like William said, there was often a tying thread. And if there was one, Doyle wanted to find it. Fast.

7

After Amanda had left to pick up Steven, her partner, Doyle and William began intensive research.

"Coffee?" asked William.

"Yes, please. With lots of sugar. This could be a really long night," said Doyle.

"You got it."

"I'm rather surprised you're not having tea, William. Are you giving up your British roots?"

"Not at all," said William. "I don't mind trying some American things. Although for lunch I tried something called 'White Castle' and I'm not so sure my digestive system will ever fully recover."

"Even Americans don't make a habit of eating White Castle," said Doyle. "Unless copious amounts of drugs are involved."

"Oh?"

"So I've heard. Anyhow, let's get back to the topic at hand. The killer my dad arrested. Is he still around?"

William's fingers rattled on the keyboard. "The man who killed Tess Sanderson was Frederick Dillman of Grand Forks. His father was the owner of a defunct pickle company that had closed its doors in 1979. Apparently Frederick Dillman still owned a warehouse full of pickles after it closed shop. He used the pickle business as a cover for introducing himself to his victims. He'd knock on their door, chat them up about his family's pickles, offer a poisoned sample, and that was that. That's how he got the moniker 'The Friendly Companion.'"

"But why do it? Just for the pleasure of killing people with pickles?" asked Doyle.

"Not necessarily. When he was arrested in 1986, the police searched his warehouse. Not only was he living there, but he had a couple hundred thousand dollars in cash stored in jars. The detectives had assumed he'd been ripping off the people he was killing."

"So was he doing it for the pleasure of killing, or the money?"

"Hard to say at this point."

"Is he alive, William?" asked Doyle.

Again, William's fingers danced across the keys. "No," he said. "He's not alive. Frederick Dillman passed away in prison in 1991. Complications from diabetes."

Doyle nodded. "Well, that's good. That eliminates the possibility that Dillman is taking care of unfinished business. Unlucky Larry's death must be unrelated."

"So it seems. But it's still an interesting connection. Nevertheless, let's turn our attention towards the basics. Someone obviously had motive to kill Larry Sanderson. But who?"

"A crazy fan? An angry ex-girlfriend?" suggested Doyle.

"Perhaps."

William turned back to the search engine and typed in "Unlucky Larry biography." A three-year-old article from the *Star Tribune* popped up titled, "Unlucky Larry finds luck in new role."

"What's all that about?"

William skimmed the article. "It's mostly about Unlucky Larry's promotion to script supervisor for *A Prairie Home Companion*. It does mention that he's been solely committed to his work since his wife passed away, although the journalist clearly decided to side-step the fact that his wife was murdered."

"Not too surprising. Go back to the search results."

William backed out of the news article. "What do you want to look at?"

"Might as well check out the Wikipedia article."

"Oh, that's never reliable."

"But still, it could be helpful."

"Very well," said William, clicking on the web link.

The article opened up, and both Doyle and William read the article all the way through.

"Huh," said Doyle. "Other than the murder of his wife, he's led a really boring life."

"Well, he was a performer. That's not too terribly boring."

"But still, nothing too interesting has happened since the murder of his wife. He never even became that successful, unless you count the fans of the show. But even they are mostly old ladies. Not so much the 'shoot somebody dead in the middle of a sold-out show' kind of crowd."

"I suppose," said William.

"The family has to know something."

"Well, if they do, hopefully Amanda and her new partner—what's the bloke's name?"

"Steven Kanter," said Doyle. "He totally hates me. Can you believe that? He hates *me*."

"I can't imagine," said William, rolling his eyes. "I've only met him the few times Amanda's brought him by. I'll be honest, I didn't get the impression he hated you. In fact, I think he was simply jealous."

Doyle considered this. "You're saying he's jealous of the fact that I have Amanda and he doesn't. I can understand that. But he tries to make one single move on my . . ."

"Actually, that's not at all what I meant. Quite the opposite. Haven't you ever noticed the way he looks—"

"Blah blah blah. Listen, I gotta catch up with Amanda. I need to seal the deal on getting us hired before Steven tries to ruin things between Amanda and myself. I finally have a fantastic girlfriend, and now other guys are trying to sneak in . . ."

"Just find out what you can about Sanderson's family, Doyle. Right?"

Doyle nodded as he set down his coffee cup and picked his keys off William's desk.

"Will do." Doyle opened the door to leave.

"And don't worry about Amanda's partner. He's obviously a—"

Doyle slammed the door behind him.

"—homosexual," William finished, resigned to the fact he was speaking to an empty room.

8

manda pulled her car along the curb near Steven's apartment in Brooklyn Park. It was dreary-looking older building. The brown paint was faded and chipped. Amanda could see plastic children's toys on the patios that looked forgotten and dirty, as though they'd seen their share of rainstorms. Instead of walking up to the door, she decided to call instead. She took out her cell phone.

"Steven, you ready to work?"

She heard a sigh. "Are you sure? It's evening. On our day off."

"We have a really exciting investigation," said Amanda. "That we're technically not assigned to. But we're going to help. Although we're not allowed to get any overtime. But we might be able to flex our schedules. But not until later this year."

"You'd make a really shitty salesperson," said Steven. "But I want to help. So I'm coming down."

"Excellent."

* * *

As Amanda drove, she filled Steven in on the situation.

"So we're delivering the next of kin notification to the daughter of the man who you saw shot on stage, even though we're not assigned to the case. Oh, and we're also attempting to help out your boyfriend, which is an obvious conflict of interest and could get us both fired. Is that right?" asked Steven, his mouth puckered as though he'd just sucked on a lemon.

"Yeah, that about sums it up. Are you okay with it, Steven? If not, I'll bring you home and you can forget we ever had this conversation. I'll completely understand and I won't hold anything against you. So, what do you say?"

Steven appeared to be weighing his options.

"Considering you're the only person in our department I get along with, I'll join you. Even though it kills me to be helping a dunderhead like McNulty. But as long as we figure everything out and make him look bad, I'm totally okay with it."

Amanda smiled. "That's great, Steven. Thank you."

"But try to get that boyfriend of yours to lighten up a little bit. He glares at me whenever I'm near you. I think he's afraid I'm going to steal you. Doesn't he realize . . . ?"

"No, he doesn't," said Amanda. "Doyle can have excellent intuition and he tends to have a good amount of luck on his side, but socially he can be rather oblivious. Usually I find it cute. Sometimes it's just sad."

Steven nodded. "Okay, well, I'm sure he'll figure it out eventually."

"He will," said Amanda.

Steven put a hand through his short, expensively trimmed hair.

"Did you just get your hair done?"

"I did. I've been going to this new stylist in uptown. He's amazing."

"No offense, but do you really have the money for that? I mean— I've seen your apartment."

Steven laughed. "I pay nothing for rent. How do you think I can afford to have fabulous haircuts, facials, manicures, pedicures, and sports massages whenever I feel like it?"

Amanda smiled. "Point taken."

"Where is this house located?"

"We just entered Golden Valley, and according to the GPS, it should be right around the corner."

"What is Doyle up to?"

"He's back at the batcave doing research with William."

"You mean the dentist office?" asked Steven.

"Yup, that's the place," said Amanda.

"But isn't that Doyle's car just up ahead?"

Amanda looked where Steven was pointing. Sure enough, it was Doyle's light blue 1995 Ford Taurus. It had some tell-tale rust spots along the rear bumper which made it easy to identify.

"Huh," said Amanda. "I guess the research went pretty quick."

Amanda pulled her Accord behind the rusted Taurus. She could see that Doyle was in the driver's seat. She got out of her car, walked up to the Taurus, and knocked on the driver's side window.

The window lowered. "Is there a problem, officer?" asked Doyle with a clever grin.

"Done with your research?" asked Amanda.

"It turned out to be a dead end," said Doyle. "Fred Dillman, the guy who killed Tess Sanderson and was eventually arrested by my dad, died in prison years ago. Which means we have to rely on Clara here," Doyle pointed at the quaint middle-class rambler, "to give us information as to who would want Larry dead."

"Then that's the information we'll get," said Amanda. "You coming in?"

Doyle looked in his rear-view mirror. "I don't want to intrude."

Amanda knew he was looking at Steven. "Doyle, really, he likes you just fine. Come with us. Seriously, you're not intruding."

Steven waved at Doyle. Doyle waved back.

"Okay, I'll come in. Just for you, Amanda."

"And also so you'll be hired and get a paycheck."

Doyle shrugged. "I guess there is some incentive, then."

Steven approached from behind. "Are we doing this?" he asked.

Amanda nodded. "Let's do it."

* * *

Doyle admired the home's professional landscaping as Steven knocked on the door. A rustling noise came from within, followed by a window curtain being pulled aside. A blond woman with bushy bangs peeked out, her eyes widening when she caught sight of the three detectives.

The door opened. "Can I help you, gentlemen?" Then the blonde saw Amanda. "And, ma'am?"

"Are you Clara Belmont?" asked Amanda.

"Oh, God," she said. She brought a hand to her forehead as if she had a headache.

"Are you okay?" asked Steven.

"It's my dad, isn't it? Something's happened?"

Doyle was about to affirm her questions when Amanda gave him a small shove against the chest. He grimaced at Amanda, but kept his mouth shut.

"Why do you think something's happened to your father, Ms. Belmont?" asked Amanda.

Clara Belmont looked apprehensively at each of the detectives. "Maybe you should come inside."

She held open the door and the detectives funneled in. She directed them to a grand, luxuriously furnished living room. Doyle could tell she must be a clean freak, because plastic covered the couch, chairs, and loveseat. Everything was in its place. It was like walking into a five-star hotel room.

"You have a nice home here, Ms. Belmont," said Doyle.

"Thanks," she said. "I know it might look like no one lives here, but my husband insists on a pristine, well-maintained home. He's working and traveling constantly, so he says I have no excuse not to keep it up." She laughed uncomfortably, then sat down on a plush-looking chair. "I'm sorry, where are my manners? Please sit."

Steven and Doyle sat on the couch, and Amanda perched on an upright recliner.

"Maybe I should have asked already, but who are you?" asked Clara Belmont.

"My name is Detective Amanda Hutchins, and this is my partner Detective Steven Kanter. We both work for the Saint Paul Police Department. We've brought along Detective Doyle Malloy as an outside resource."

"Then I was right. It must be something pretty serious if you're bringing in outside resources."

This time Amanda provided a slight nod, but reiterated the question, "Why did you automatically assume this was about your dad, Ms. Belmont?"

"Well," she said, taking a deep breath, "a couple weeks ago, my sister Tabby called from Minot. She said there was an article in the McLean County newspaper about Unlucky Larry . . . you know, my dad, suddenly passing away. Tabby wanted to know why no one had told her about Dad's death. I was eating lunch with Dad at the time, and he was even more shocked to find out he'd died. When I passed the phone over to him, I could almost hear screams of joy all the way from Minot."

"Where did the paper get their information?" asked Doyle.

"That's the funny thing," said Clara. "We called the paper, and the man whose name appears on the article claims he didn't know the first thing about it. No one took any responsibility. It was like someone intentionally snuck the article into the newspaper. How does that happen?"

"How did your father react to the story?" asked Amanda.

"He took it as a sign that someone was out to get him."

"Why?" asked Amanda.

"Well, you have to realize that he always felt that way. After Mom died . . . er . . . you know, was murdered," Clara cleared her throat, "and even after the man was put away in prison, Dad still seemed on edge. He was so used to being with Mom, I think after she was gone, he was half hoping someone would jump out of the woodwork and take him out too. I know that sounds sick, but that's what Dad was like. I thought after the murderer died in prison Dad might get better, but if anything it just made his paranoia worse."

A brief moment of silence followed. Doyle moved uncomfortably in his seat, and the movement caused a loud squeak on the plastic chair covering.

Clara shot Doyle a dirty look.

"Sorry. Amanda made *huevos rancheros* this morning."

Amanda closed her eyes and grimaced.

"Just kidding," said Doyle. "Please, go on."

Clara looked as though she'd lost her train of thought. Then she shook her head and continued. "Anyway, I guess he had reason to be paranoid, huh? What happened? How did it happen?"

"On stage," said Doyle. "He was shot several times. He died instantly."

Clara nodded. Then she broke into tears. Her previously reserved face gave way to waterfalls. "I'm sorry. Just give me a minute."

Doyle searched for a box of tissues, and not seeing any, found a bathroom down the hall. He tore off a long strip of toilet paper then headed back to the couch, handing Clara the toilet paper before he sat down. Again, the couch made an unpleasant sound, but no one reacted this time.

Clara dabbed her eyes with the toilet paper. "Do you know who—"

"We don't have any suspects yet," said Amanda. "Which is why we're trying to understand his background. Did he have any enemies?"

Clara shook her head. "No, not that I'm aware of. Really, he was just a funny showman. Other than his performances, he kept mostly to himself. I really don't know who would want to kill him."

"Here's the situation, Clara," said Amanda. "The case is currently assigned to Detectives McNulty and Jenkins. They'll be leading the case, and, chances are, you'll be seeing one of them on the news tomorrow morning delivering a press release. Detective Kanter and myself will assist all we can, although we'll likely be assigned to other cases in the meantime."

"Why are you here then?" asked Clara.

"Other than notifying you of what happened to your father, we wanted to give you the option of hiring Detective Malloy to lead a separate investigation. He works privately, meaning he has a lot more capabilities than the Saint Paul PD has, and he would be dedicated to finding the killer full time. It's simply an extra option you're under no obligation to consider."

Clara looked at Doyle. "Are you good?"

Doyle nodded. "I've solved a lot of cases," he said. "And you wouldn't just be hiring me, but my entire staff. Like Detective Hutchins said, we'd be on this investigation full time. You don't have to decide now. But if you decide this needs more attention than you're getting from the police, then please consider me. I'd be happy to help."

Doyle handed Clara his business card.

"Okay, but I'd like to think about it. I need time to get my head straight."

"That's fine," said Doyle. "But don't wait too long. Often the most important investigation happens within the first forty-eight hours."

"So I've heard. I watch a lot of TV. There's really not much else to do with my husband gone so much."

Doyle held out his hand. "Call anytime. I'm always up."

Clara shook his hand. "Okay. Thanks."

Amanda and Steven stood up, and Doyle followed suit.

"Thank you so much for your help, Ms. Belmont," said Steven. "We're so sorry for your loss."

"I appreciate it you coming out to tell me in person," said Clara. "It means a lot."

"Not a problem, ma'am," said Steven.

"Just let me know if there are any developments," said Clara. "Anything at all, I'd like to know."

"Absolutely," said Steven.

Doyle pulled his rusted Ford Taurus into the parking lot of the retirement community that he called home. In his early forties, Doyle Malloy was hardly retirement age, but the condos were cheap, the location was good, and lucky for Amanda, there wasn't another female under the age of sixty that could be considered competition for Doyle's affections.

At first, Doyle was been hesitant to let Amanda move in with him. He was afraid he'd be giving up a lot of what made him . . . *him*. But to his shock, she didn't try to change him. His original light saber replicas still hung in the living room. Classic movie posters still adorned the bedroom wall. She was an addition to his life, not a subtraction. He couldn't put into words how much that meant to him.

When Steven came into the picture, Doyle got his first real taste of jealousy. He'd never felt that way before, but he knew what it meant. Amanda was the world to him, and there was no way he was going to let another man sneak his way into Amanda's heart. Even if, God forbid, Doyle had to get tough and defend his territory.

Doyle walked up to the doorway where just two years prior, Kimberly Chapman, the gorgeous daughter of acclaimed actor Timothy Chapman, had been waiting for Doyle to return so she could give him information. He didn't even realize at the time that she'd broken his door knob trying to get in. He just recently got around to getting the damned thing fixed. But still, as attractive as Kimberly Chapman was, she was nothing compared to the intelligence, courage, and heart that exuded from Amanda every single day.

As Doyle walked in, his phone rang. "Doyle here."

"Doyle, it's William. Please tell me you're near your computer."

"I just walked in. Let me fire it up."

Doyle sat down at his computer and interrupted the screensaver, which happened to be a photo of Doyle and Josh Hartnett on the set of *Fargo 2: Midwest Bugaloo*, a film that, due to various legal and criminal reasons, was unlikely to ever see the light of day.

"Are you on your computer yet?" asked William.

"Hold on, hold on—it's a Gateway. These things take time."

"Just let me know when it's up. I'm just going to e-mail you a few files right now."

"Sure, William. Just about there. What's happening?"

"I haven't seen anything on the news here, but as soon as I went online and looked for information on that Sanderson family, I couldn't help but see the current events in North Dakota. And good heavens, Doyle— several murders have taken place in North Dakota in the past year."

"Okay, I'll grant you that murder isn't too common in North Dakota, William, but it doesn't necessarily mean there's anything connected to Larry Sanderson's murder. Were these North Dakota victims all shot on stage? That'd be pretty astounding."

"No, nothing like that," said William. "Can you see your e-mail?"

"I'm opening it right now."

"Take a look at the first photo I sent you," said William. "It's labeled 'Bismarck #1.'"

"Okay, I just opened it," said Doyle. "What am I looking at here?"

"Ms. Hilga Johansen was murdered in her home in Bismarck four months ago. It appeared to be poison, but the authorities haven't pinpointed where the poison originated. Her safe had been broken into and her money stolen as well."

Doyle nodded, even though William wasn't there to witness it. "I'll grant you, that does sound an awful lot like Fred Dillman's modus operandi, but he's dead, William."

"Perhaps it's just a coincidence?" asked William. "After all, coincidences can happen, right?"

"But you don't believe in coincidences."

"Bloody well right. Look at the photo. You can see Ms. Johansen on the floor of her kitchen. The cupboards are on one side of her, and you can see the pantry in the background."

"Okay, I see that," said Doyle.

"Do you see anything unusual?"

Doyle continued to look at the photo. "No, I don't see—"

"Look at 'Bismarck #2.'"

"Okay," said Doyle, opening the file. "What am I looking at here?"

"I blew up the image of the pantry. What do you see?"

Doyle studied the image. He was about to say he didn't see anything when suddenly something caught his eye. "I'll be damned. Dillman's Original Kosher Dills."

"Doyle, that brand hasn't been around since the late 1970s, long before Fred Dillman began his murderous rampage. If you recall, Fred Dillman used his defunct family brand as a cover. It seems whoever is committing these murders is using the same cover."

"Oh, this is bad, William. This is really, really bad."

"I know," said William.

"This brings up too many questions. Is this a copycat? Is it someone else from the Dillman family? Or were two people working together in the 1980s, and the lone partner decided to pick up where they'd left off? Or, and I really hate to think this . . ."

"Did your father arrest the wrong person?" asked William. "That's really your biggest concern, I'm certain. And it's a valid one. But let's not worry about that until we learn more."

"I suppose," said Doyle.

"Are you ready to go?"

"What? Go where?"

"North Dakota, obviously. I highly doubt a serial killer is going to turn himself in. And there's certainly no guarantee the North Dakota police will manage. Not to mention I doubt the FBI is even aware of the nature of these killings. This is all on us, Doyle."

"But this might not have anything to do with Larry Sanderson's murder. That's what we're working on now. Not a serial killer in North Dakota. I'm not prepared to deal with a serial killer. I have absolutely no experience in that area. If the killer was a celebrity, like Kevin Sorbo, then I might be able to help. Otherwise, I'm way out of my league."

"Who? Never mind. Settle down, Doyle. I'll be there to help. Besides, it will be good experience for you."

"Listen. Amanda will be home soon after she drops Steven off. I can't just head out to North Dakota without talking to her first."

Doyle heard a sigh.

"Very well, Doyle. Think about it. But I'll tell you this. I'm leaving at 10:00 o'clock tomorrow morning, with or without you. I do hope you'll be with me."

"I'll call you in the morning." Doyle hung up.

It'd already been a long night, and Doyle could already tell it was going to turn into a very long week.

10

Doyle woke to the unpleasant sensation of Amanda slapping his face repeatedly.

"Wake up, wake up, wake up," said Amanda.

"Ow, that really hurts," said Doyle, rubbing his tingling skin. "What's so important that you had to wake me up from an incredibly pleasant dream about Scarlett Johansson in a pool of Jello pudding?"

Amanda slapped him again.

"Ow! All right, what is it?" Doyle blinked. He could tell from the light pouring in that it was early morning.

"Just watch the news," said Amanda, pointing to the TV on the wall opposite their bed. "McNulty's been delivering a press conference."

"This should be good," said Doyle. He grabbed the remote and turned up the volume.

"And so, long story short, Lucky Garry was shot dead and we're following up on all leads. Anyone who has information should contact the Saint Paul Police Department. Information leading to an arrest may or may not result in a reward of some sort. Questions?"

The audience of media members scrambled to get their questions out first, but were treated to an abrupt, *"No questions? Well, then—we'll provide further information as it becomes available. Good day."*

"Wow," said Doyle. "He didn't even call him by his correct stage name. Though I'm not surprised. McNulty is definitely more brawn than brain."

"You got that right," said Amanda. "Assuming Clara Belmont was watching, she should be calling you in no time."

"Now we're in business, baby!" said Doyle. "I need some Count Chocula."

Doyle rolled out of bed and began to stretch when his cell phone rang.

"Do you think that's her?" asked Amanda.

"It might be," said Doyle, picking up the phone. He looked at the screen, but he didn't recognize the number.

"Doyle Malloy, Private Detective," he answered.

"Mr. Malloy, this is Chief Cynthia Reiser with the Saint Paul Police Department."

"Ms. Razor . . . er, Reiser, that is. How can I be of assistance?"

Amanda's eyes widened at the mention Reiser's name. She searched for her own phone, looking in the pockets of her jeans that lay on the floor as well as the pockets of her coat that hung on the closet door.

Doyle realized the call from Chief Reiser probably wasn't to seek Doyle's expertise in detection.

"You're listed as Amanda Hutchins emergency contact and I've been *trying* to get ahold of her all morning."

"I see," said Doyle. "I understand she's been having technology issues with her mobile phone. I'll make sure she contacts you as soon as she can."

"Don't bother with that," said Reiser. "Just tell her to get her ass to my office immediately."

"Will do," said Doyle.

"Mr. Malloy, why don't you join her. I want to speak with you as well."

"Um, sure. Yeah, no problem. We'll be right in."

Amanda looked like her head was about to burst like a piñata.

"I mean, Amanda will be there," said Doyle backtracking, although Amanda still didn't seem pleased. "That is, if she can. Which, I think she can . . ." Amanda was shaking her head, "but maybe she can't, in which case I'll come in . . ." Now Amanda was waving her hands and shaking her head simultaneously. "But not without Amanda, because that's who you really want to see, right?"

Amanda covered her face with her hands.

"Mr. Malloy, I have no idea what kind of detective you are and what your relationship is with Amanda. But make damn sure you're here with Detective Hutchins within thirty minutes, or she can look for a new job and I'll arrest you for interfering with an investigation."

"Interfering with—?" Doyle would have questioned this further, but Chief Reiser had already hung up.

Amanda looked worried. "What the hell just happened?"

"I don't think that call went very well," said Doyle.

"We're going downtown, aren't we?"

"Yup."

"Shit. This can't be good."

* * *

"I suppose you know why I called you in here," said Chief Cynthia Reiser. Doyle could tell why she was nicknamed Razor. While her spoken language wasn't all too intimidating, her piercing eyes reflected the anger behind them.

"Well," said Amanda, composing herself, "I assume you want Steven and me to take on a stronger role in this Unlucky Larry case. McNulty and Jenkins are great at what they do, but such a highly-scrutinized crime as this one is going to require—"

"That's not why you're here," said Reiser. "Not by a long shot."

Reiser rose from her chair. Her height, or lack thereof, surprised Doyle. He now understood what kind of a woman they were dealing with. Her chair was on a raised platform, giving her the appearance of being much taller behind her desk. The office was her kingdom and this was her throne. Doyle wondered if he should be kneeling.

"Perhaps I could suggest something," said Doyle.

"No," said Reiser. "You may not. You're here only to listen. Understand?"

Doyle didn't respond.

"Do you understand?" repeated Reiser.

"Umm, you told me not to talk."

Amanda turned her head and glared at him.

"A smart guy," said Reiser under her breath. "I hate dealing with smart guys. I'm sure you think you're really damn clever, Mr. Malloy. In fact, I think both of you think you're clever. Isn't that right, Detective Hutchins?"

"Chief, listen . . . we were only trying to help last night by notifying Clara Belmont of her father's death. It seemed like McNulty and Jenkins were plenty busy with the crime scene, and we only wanted to offer an extra hand. That's it."

"That's it," repeated Reiser. "You had absolutely no other motive for going to Clara Belmont's house last night?"

Both Doyle and Amanda shook their heads.

Reiser sat down on her desk and leaned towards Doyle and Amanda, bringing her face within a few feet of theirs.

"Then tell me why I received a call at seven o'clock this morning from Ms. Belmont asking why our city's police force is so unskilled and unprepared to deal with a homicide investigation that the very detectives who should be solving her father's murder are instead soliciting her to hire an amateur private detective. A detective who, according to her statement, allegedly has far more resources and capabilities than the entire Saint Paul police force. Is that what you led her to believe, Mr. Malloy?"

"No, no, no," said Doyle. "That's not right at all. I only wanted her to contact me if she had any additional information. Like Amanda—"

Reiser's steely eyes flashed.

"Err, like Detective Hutchins, that is, was saying . . . we only wanted to help. Honestly."

"Honestly," Reiser repeated. "I really wish you hadn't said that, Mr. Malloy. Because I don't trust you. And right now, Detective Hutchins, I'm afraid I don't trust you either."

Amanda's face slackened. Doyle thought she might get sick.

"I'm sorry, Chief. I had no intentions of getting in the way of this investigation or . . . causing you to lose confidence in me. That's the last thing I want."

"You're an excellent investigator, Ms. Hutchins. When you came over from Minneapolis, I wasn't sure how well you'd do. Especially in such a male-dominated department. But you've been effective and successful. So far."

Doyle and Amanda looked uncomfortably at each other.

"Let me get right down to saying what I need to say," said Chief Reiser, returning to her throne. She sat down and crossed her arms. Her look was cold. Hard. Calculating.

"Detective Hutchins, I'm suspending you for one week without pay."

Amanda emitted a quiet groan.

"Your partner, Detective Kanter, is also being suspended but with pay. Reason being, I believe he followed along with whatever you two had cooked up and didn't want to cause a rift with his new partner. I can appreciate that, but he still needs to learn where his loyalties lie, as do you, Ms. Hutchins."

Doyle glanced over to see how Amanda was handling the news, but she didn't look back at him. Her head was down.

"Mr. Malloy, I have no direct power over you, although I do have influence. Let me make this clear. If you remain involved in this case in any capacity, I'll make absolutely certain that you don't have any friends here willing to help you out in the future. You'll become a leper to us. An outcast. That could be devastating to your career. I'm sure you exchange information with cops all the time, and vice versa. I'll see that comes to an end. Do I make myself clear?"

Doyle nodded.

"Amanda," said Reiser. Amanda looked up. "Same goes for you. If you are involved in this investigation in any capacity, you'll be terminated. Furthermore, if you attempt to solicit work for your *boyfriend*," Reiser paused and looked at Doyle demurely, "during the process of any investigation whatsoever, whether it be during or after business hours, you will be terminated. Is that perfectly clear?"

Amanda nodded. "Yes, Chief."

Reiser's expression changed. She now looked at Amanda with sympathy. "Really use this next week. Think of what this job means to you. Think of where you were two years ago . . . behind the reception desk of the MPD. Now you're a homicide investigator for Saint Paul. That's quite an accomplishment. Don't throw it away."

Amanda nodded. "Okay."

"You may leave now," said Reiser. "Go."

That was pleasant," said Doyle. They were sitting in the Rabbit Hole, a coffee shop run by Shay O'Hanlon, Doyle's first girlfriend. Before Shay began dating girls. Doyle still assumed his inadequacies and lack of skill had turned her.

The car ride from Saint Paul to Minneapolis had been long, silent, and excruciating. Doyle checked his watch. It was 9:30. *William's leaving soon*, he thought.

"What are you thinking about?" asked Doyle. This was one of those tense relationship moments that Doyle had never been comfortable with, and usually it was a precursor to a break-up. Doyle wasn't going to let that happen if he could help it.

"She's right, you know," said Amanda, looking at him sadly. "It's a conflict of interest. I shouldn't be trying to get you work when I'm the one who should be able to do it myself. And the thing is . . . I know I can do it myself. And I have a great partner who can do it with me."

"Don't bring up Steven," Doyle said, too abruptly.

"Why? Feeling jealous?"

Doyle calmed himself. "It's not that. I just don't want you two getting close. Maybe that is jealousy. I don't know. Maybe I'm still afraid of losing you."

Amanda was caught off guard. She choked back a sob. "You're not going to, Doyle. This is just a speed bump. But that doesn't change the fact that we have to start approaching things in a new way. I can't solicit work for you. We have to run our investigations separately. You can't benefit from a case I'm working on."

Doyle nodded. "I get that. Maybe we were crossing the line."

Shay returned to their table and topped off their coffees. "You know what they say," said Shay. "You can try to see how close to the line you can get without crossing it, only to discover the line is a mile behind you."

"You were eavesdropping," said Doyle.

"Obviously," said Shay. "It's a coffee shop. All I do all day is make coffee and listen to people's chatter."

"And offer sage-like advice," said Amanda.

"Sometimes," said Shay. "Listen, if you want any advice, this is what I have to offer. Don't let other people decide for you what's in your best interest. Do what you feel you need to do. If you two are afraid about crossing a line, then move the line. Erase it. Draw a new one. It's up to you."

Doyle was confounded at first, then impressed. Shay's advice made a lot of sense.

"Thanks, Shay," said Doyle. "Thanks a bunch."

Shay smiled. "You got it. By the way, scones are half off till noon. We're overstocked."

"Good to know."

Amanda quizzically looked at Doyle. "So what did you take from that piece of advice?"

"We should go to North Dakota," said Doyle.

"Come again?"

"Remember the e-mails I told you about last night? The ones from William? This is a chance to make our own rules. Do our own thing," said Doyle.

"Whoa, not a chance. You heard what Razor said. Anything related to the investigation and I'm fired and you'll be run out of town."

Doyle shook his head. "It's not related. Fred Dillman is dead. The man who killed Larry's wife is dead. Larry was shot. Whoever is killing people in North Dakota with Dillman brand pickles obviously wouldn't have shot Larry because that's not the killer's M.O. Unrelated cases."

"Then why go? We're not hired by anyone. Why do it?"

"To stop a serial killer," said Doyle.

"That's all well and good, but we've never dealt with a serial killer before."

"I know. But what a great time to start!"

"Wait a minute," said Amanda, eyes widening. "There is a connection. You think your father might have gotten the wrong guy. If he did, then the cases could be related."

Doyle sighed. "I'll grant you, I'd like to know if my dad actually caught the right person. But even if he didn't, the cases are still separate. The M.O. It's different. The only thread linking these situations is the death of Tess Sanderson. That doesn't appear to have any relevance on Larry's murder."

"What about William?"

"He's going regardless of what we do. This is what he used to do as a career back in London. William is practically a serial killer hunter. He'll probably nab the guy five minutes after crossing the state line."

Amanda smiled. "I can totally understand why you'd want to do this. And I'll admit—it's kind of exciting."

"And you have some free time on your hands."

"No thanks to you," said Amanda.

"It was kinda your idea that—"

Amanda shot him an evil Medusa look.

"You know what? Never mind. Not important."

Amanda's expression softened. "Okay, let's say for argument's sake that we actually go to North Dakota to catch a killer. What if we discover there's a connection to Unlucky Larry's murder?"

"Then we stop what we're doing, hightail it out of North Dakota, and pretend like we were in our apartment making sweet, sweet love during the course of the week."

"Wouldn't you rather just do that instead?" asked Amanda.

"Eh, we've done plenty of that already."

Amanda playfully scowled at him.

"What do you think? Feel like saving a whole lot of people from dying at the hands of a pickle-pushing pillager of people's personal property and pulmonary performance?"

"Dear God. Were you working on that all night?"

"A little," said Doyle. "Too much?"

"A little."

"So . . . ?"

"Okay, let's do it. Call William. Tell him we're coming." Amanda reached in her coat pocket and pulled out her cell phone.

"Who are you calling?"

"Steven."

"No, not a chance. He can't come with."

"I only want to give him the opportunity," said Amanda. "Besides, I'm not sure what you're getting all worked up about. He's gay, after all."

"You listen here, Amanda—I flat out . . . wait, what?"

Amanda rolled her eyes. "Really? You haven't seen the way he looks at you?"

"What? Like he wants to kill me so he can have you all to himself?"

"Kinda, except the other way around."

"So you're saying . . . oh. Oh," repeated Doyle. "I get it. I guess I'll take that as a compliment. He likes me. Huh."

"Don't get any funny ideas, Malloy. You're still mine. I don't want you switching teams this far into the relationship."

"I'm good," said Doyle. "No need to worry. But I feel a whole heck of a lot better about Steven, now. I was afraid I'd have to get in a fist fight with that guy."

"It could still happen if you bother him enough. You have that way with people you know."

"I have no idea what you're talking about. But anyway, go ahead and call Steven. He's okay in my book."

"Good."

"Listen, do you mind if I head down to the Martiniapolis? It'll take me five minutes," said Doyle.

"You want a drink now? It's only 9:45 in the morning."

"I'm not getting a drink, but I know who will be as soon as it turns 10:00. I want to see if Hanratty will join us."

"Oh, Doyle—I don't know."

"It'll be fine. I promise. I'm not sure if he'll want to go, but I should at least offer. Besides, I'll call William and tell him to give us another twenty minutes."

"If you insist," said Amanda.

Doyle stood and kissed Amanda on the lips. He pulled away, hesitated, then leaned in for one more.

Amanda obliged, then smiled.

"I'll see you in a few minutes," said Doyle. "Then it's time to pack."

12

When Doyle stepped inside the Martiniapolis from the bright morning, the tavern seemed especially dim. It was one of those buildings that had been around forever, although it'd gone through many name changes over the years. The smoking ban had been enforced some years ago, but smoke still clung to the walls and floor, much like the tavern's patrons after too many drinks. Tiny bits of popcorn crunched under Doyle's shoes as he made his way to the bar, where he noticed a familiar face.

"Officer Glenn Hanratty," said Doyle, holding out his closed fist.

The rail thin man at the bar completed the fist bump, then let his hand fall limply to the countertop.

"We have to work on your fist-bumping skills, Hanratty. Your hand should explode, not fall down like a ballerina who stubbed her toe."

"I really don't care, Doyle," said Hanratty, taking a drink from his glass of beer. "And you called me 'Officer.' I wish you wouldn't do that. You know damn well I haven't worked since the MPD cleaned house."

"I know, I know," said Doyle. "Do you still blame me for that?"

"Of course," said Hanratty. "If you'd let the Chief of Police get away with fraud, conspiracy to commit murder, aggravated assault, and conduct unbecoming of a police officer, I'd be just fine." Hanratty smiled.

"Very funny," said Doyle. "So you've gotten over it?"

"Yeah, yeah. I don't blame you. They would have gotten rid of me sooner or later. They don't have much tolerance for alcoholics nowadays."

"Oh, please," said Doyle. "Every cop drinks."

"Sure, but not every cop totals his squad car, gets assigned to work as a bike cop, then has no less than three police-issued Schwinns stolen."

"How does that even happen?"

"Leaving them unattended in front of an establishment such as this," said Hanratty.

"You didn't lock them?"

"Nah. I figured no one would want a cop bike. I sure as hell didn't."

A bartender approached Doyle.

"Mornin', Terry," said Doyle. "You look tired."

"Long night. You want the usual?" the bartender asked.

Doyle nodded. Within seconds, the blender was whirring.

"So are you doing okay, Hanratty?"

Hanratty shrugged. "My unemployment benefits have run out, but I'm making some money on Ebay. I've been hitting a lot of garage sales."

"That's . . . good," said Doyle.

"It's better than watching *Maury* in my underwear all day."

"I'll give you that."

"So what are you doing here, Doyle? This isn't your usual time of day to show up. You're more of an evening after-work kinda drinker. Not a 'oh, good, another shitty day, guess I'll go to the bar' kinda drinker."

The bartender placed the blue frozen beverage in front of Doyle and began to walk away.

"Whoa, whoa, whoa," said Doyle.

The bartender turned around and rolled his bloodshot eyes. Then he reached under the bar, brought out a small, frilly umbrella, and placed it in Doyle's drink.

"Thank you, good sir," said Doyle.

The bartender grunted and stalked off.

Doyle sucked a healthy amount of blueberry daiquiri through the straw. "Mmm, perfection."

"That's just sad," said Hanratty. "You really need to upgrade from the girlie drinks."

"There's nothing girlie about this drink," said Doyle. "It can give you one heck of a cold headache."

Hanratty just shook his head.

"Anyhow, the reason I'm here, Hanratty, is to see if you have anything going on the next few days."

Hanratty looked at Doyle quizzically. "Well, I'm not sure, Doyle. I'll have to consult with my secretary, maybe reschedule some important meetings . . . then there's all that paperwork to do . . ."

"You don't have a secretary," said Doyle, taking another sip.

Hanratty rubbed his forehead. "I know that, Doyle. What do you have in mind for me? I'm pretty open."

"Well, I'm about to head out for North Dakota, and I thought—"

"No way," said Hanratty.

"But you didn't let me—"

"I'm not going to North Dakota," said Hanratty.

"Why not?"

"Corn. Wheat. Sugar beets."

"So?"

"Miles of them! It doesn't end! Seeing a cow should *not* be the most exciting part of a road trip."

"So you don't want to go?"

"No," said Hanratty, crossing his arms across his chest.

"Even if I pay you?"

"You want to pay me to go to North Dakota?" Hanratty raised his eyebrows.

"Yes," said Doyle. "What do you think of that?"

"This will officially be the hardest decision I've ever made."

"Don't be so melodramatic. Here's the deal. Me, William, Amanda, and possibly her new partner Steven are heading out soon. We're tracking down a serial killer who appears to be a copycat of the Friendly Companion from the 1980s."

"Really? The Friendly Companion?"

"Yes, you're familiar with him?" asked Doyle.

"Yeah, he's the pickle guy, right?"

"Exactly," said Doyle.

"So is the copycat killing people with pickles?"

"From what we've seen in photographs, yes, it appears so."

"Is there an investigation in place? Are you doing this with Amanda in an official capacity?"

"No," said Doyle. "So far, it appears the police have not made the connection between the copycat and the Friendly Companion. The only reason William found out was because we'd just been discussing my father's first big arrest, the one that made his career, and there happened to be a loose connection to another situation we'd been looking at."

"Another situation? Are there two simultaneous cases going on here?"

"No, no, no—definitely not," said Doyle. "And as far as Amanda is concerned, there is absolutely no other case, okay? No matter how much you hear about Unlucky Larry in the news—"

"Unlucky Larry? Are you seriously saying there's a connection between Unlucky Larry's on-stage murder and the copycat pickle murderer?"

The bartender eyed Doyle and Hanratty suspiciously.

"This is private business, Terry. Also, I would like some peanuts."

The bartender shook his head and brought Doyle a bowl of nuts.

Doyle lowered his voice and responded to Hanratty. "No, no I did not say that. And there is absolutely no evidence there is a connection of any sort."

"But you think there is," said Hanratty.

Doyle hesitated. Hanratty grinned.

"Well, what do you think, Hanratty? Can you handle a lot of corn, wheat, and sugar beets?"

"Sure, but throw in a few dead bodies, and it's a lot more interesting. What are you paying me for, exactly?"

"Do you still have your photography equipment?" asked Doyle.

"Sure. Whenever the MPD bought new equipment, they'd sell me the old stuff dirt cheap. I've almost got a complete darkroom in my apartment."

"That's kind of creepy."

"I don't do any nudes," said Hanratty. "So, you're saying you want me to document everything on this trip, is that right? How exactly are you getting paid?"

"I haven't figured that part out yet. But that's not really the point. We have a chance to stop a serial killer. And I want to know what, if anything, this might have to do with my dad's first big arrest."

"Fair enough," said Hanratty. "Okay, when do we leave?" Hanratty took a sip of his beer.

"In about twenty minutes," said Doyle.

Hanratty sprayed his beer all over the counter. "Come again?"

"Sorry. I realize this might be short notice."

"You think?" Hanratty shook his head, reached down to his back pocket, and pulled out his wallet.

"No, no, I got this one."

"Oh, thanks, Doyle," said Hanratty.

"Don't thank me too much," said Doyle. "We're going to keep the drinking to a minimum the next few days."

Hanratty glared at Doyle. "You're lucky you said 'minimum' instead of 'cold turkey.'"

"I wanted to make sure you'd come with."

"Smart man," said Hanratty, draining the last of his beer.

Doyle left enough cash on the bar to pay for both of their drinks.

"Can I at least go home and get some clothes to bring?" asked Hanratty.

"Sure, just meet us at our office when you're ready."

"You mean the dentist office?"

"Exactly."

"That sounds great, Doyle. But do you know what would be even better?"

"What's that?"

"If you gave me a ride."

Doyle chuckled. "You got it."

PART III

September, 2012

I-94 to North Dakota

If you've reached the World's Largest Buffalo sculpture, you've gone too far.

13

The Friendly Companion pulled into the driveway of the small, one-story rambler in Valley City, just sixty miles west of Fargo. He licked his lips. His mouth was dry.

He called himself the Friendly Companion, even though no one else was calling him that yet. Once they caught on to what he was up to, he knew what word they'd be using. *Copycat*. He hated that word. It was condescending.

He opened the glove box and pulled out two black leather gloves. Sliding the gloves on reminded him of each of his victims. Every murder he'd committed began this way. Each one killed for the greater good. What the police and media weren't smart enough to appreciate yet was that he was creating a character. That foolish tool Dillman had something special and didn't even realize it. Sure, he stole some money from some elderly folks and committed a few murders in the process, but the media came up with the idea of the Friendly Companion. Dillman could have ran with it. He could have made the Friendly Companion a legend, something children feared at night. A midwestern Chupacabra.

But Dillman had been stupid and got caught. Way too early. But fortunately he had some secrets just waiting to be exploited.

And now the Friendly Companion was going to be far bigger than Fred Dillman could have imagined.

Stepping out of the car, he stretched. The long drive had stiffened his muscles terribly. He walked around to the rear passenger door and grabbed a tan canvas workbag.

He looked around. It was nearly a quarter mile to the next house. That's why he loved these small towns. Screaming wouldn't be an issue.

He studied his reflection in the car window. His business suit, overcoat, and gloves made him look exactly like a well-to-do insurance salesman on a brisk September day. With his handsome looks and inviting smile, he looked downright friendly.

Walking up to the door, he took some paperwork out of his bag. It was insurance information he'd ordered over the phone from one of those commercials that aired during old-people shows, like *The Price Is Right*. He didn't know a thing about insurance.

When he pulled out the paperwork, the small jar of pickles almost rolled out right onto the cement walkway. Christ almighty, that would have been a grievous mistake. There were very few of these jars left in existence, and he didn't have a back-up with him in his car. He almost had to scrap a whole day's work.

He knocked on the door. Just as expected, a little old lady answered.

"Can I help you?" she asked, adjusting the wire-rimmed glasses below her snow-white bangs. She kept the thin screen door shut and spoke through it.

"Are you Ms. Madeline Benson?" he asked, showing off his pearly whites.

"Yes, sir, but everyone calls me Maddie."

"Well, Maddie, do you mind if I come in and talk to you for a few minutes?"

"That depends. I'm not really interested in that Mormon faith, if that's what you're peddling. No offense, of course. I'm a life-long Lutheran, and I'm too gosh-darned old and stubborn to change that now."

"No, ma'am. This is actually about an insurance policy your husband had taken out on himself."

"Stan? Oh, I collected on that policy two years ago after he passed, God rest his soul."

"This is a different one." The Friendly Companion held up the paperwork in his hand.

He could hear her turn the squeaky handle of the screen door, but then she hesitated. "Where are you from?"

"Well, I'm originally from Chicago. I spent most of my life there, but I moved to the Twin Cities after college. I have family in North Dakota, so I always enjoy getting out to your fine state whenever I have a chance."

"That's real nice, but I meant which company? What insurance company is located in the Twin Cities, and why drive all the way out here?"

"Um, RiverSource, ma'am."

Maddie Benson squinted and held her glasses firmly in place. "Then why does it say MetLife on your paperwork there?"

His smile disappeared, replaced with fury. He grabbed the screen door's knob and yanked with all his strength. Maddie had been holding the knob on the other side, and she stumbled forward with the door. She practically fell into his arms. He responded with a violent shove, knocking her back into the house. She landed with a thud on the beige carpet.

She attempted to scream, but he was on her too fast. His leather-clad hands closed around her throat. One of the very first sales tactics he'd learned years ago was to go all the way. Close the deal.

She managed to croak out two words. "It's okay."

He expected to see fear in her eyes, but instead he only saw complacency and acceptance. He didn't like that, not one bit. The rage swept through him like lightning, causing him to squeeze even tighter. He didn't know for how long. He lost track. But there was no struggle.

She was already gone.

He released his grip from the lifeless body below him. His workbag was lying in the entryway. It'd fallen off his shoulder during the struggle. He reached in to grab the jar of pickles, but instead pulled his hand away with a sliced leather glove and a stinging pain in the palm of his hand.

Broken glass. The jar had broken after all. He couldn't place the jar in the pantry like he'd planned.

Shit.

He felt the anger brewing inside him, but reason quickly pacified him. It already upset him that the police were too stupid to realize a serial killer was on the loose, a killer that just happened to be the Friendly Companion. Well, at last they'll figure it out soon enough.

He held up the workbag with his injured hand and reached into it with his uncut hand and carefully plucked out a pickle, being careful to avoid the shards of glass. While he avoided getting cut, he inadvertently knocked the workbag on its side, allowing the loose pickle juice to run freely onto his pants. "Oh, no," he said.

It wasn't simple embarrassment. The Friendly Companion had a condition. An allergy. The irony of this particular allergy was not lost on him. His body immediately began to react to the pickle juice. He felt the intense itch, like an angry badger gnawing at his crotch.

He scratched and scratched and scratched. The pain blossomed like a rose with many thorns. Limping and scratching, he walked over to Maddie Benson's body, knelt down, and shoved the pickle into her mouth.

He hoped this would clue in the police.

The Friendly Companion looked back at his workbag. He decided one extra detail would help. He went back into the bag, being extremely careful to avoid getting any further pickle juice onto himself. He took out two shards of glass that were connected by a lime-green label. Dillman's Original Kosher Dills. He dropped the shards of glass onto Maddie Benson's chest.

"That oughtta do it," he said to himself. The cops would put the pieces together. They'd be on his tail soon. That was okay. He only had a couple more planned, then he'd stop. He'd give it up until people stopped talking about him. Until they forgot. Then he'd be back.

The Friendly Companion picked up his workbag which was soaked with pickle juice and headed towards the door. Then he dropped it, not only to scratch his genitals again, but because he was amazed by his own forgetfulness.

He turned back around, then began to search for Maddie Benson's fifty thousand dollars.

14

"Remind me again why we're here?" asked William with distaste as he observed the décor of the unusual restaurant they were eating in.

"This is probably the most amazing themed restaurant in the entire Midwest," said Doyle. "Space Aliens is a landmark. You can't possibly travel through Fargo without stopping in."

"I like it," said Steven. "It's geek chic. That's really been in style the last couple years."

Amanda looked at Doyle and raised her eyebrow as if to say, *Really? You didn't know?*

"This place is ridiculous," said William. "It's gaudy and unattractive, there's far too much neon, I don't much care for the fellow walking around in an alien costume, and the names of the menu items are absolutely dreadful. Wings from Planet X. Jalapeno Rockets. Space Fries. Bloody hell."

"Say what you will, the Space Ribs are delicious. Out of this world, even," said Doyle, laughing to himself.

"Can I at least have a Cosmic Lemonade?" asked Hanratty, looking uncomfortable.

"It's loaded with alcohol," said Doyle. "I don't think that's a good idea."

"Fine," he said disdainfully. "I'll keep drinking soda then."

Doyle wiped his hands on a napkin. "Beyond just enjoying this meal, I wanted to go over our game plan. We've taken two vehicles, so I think it makes sense to split up and cover as much ground as we can."

Doyle saw nods of approval and continued.

"This copycat is covering a large area. Dillman stuck mostly to western North Dakota, but this new killer is covering the whole state. I think we should split our groups into east and west."

"What about police involvement?" asked Steven. "It would feel wrong to investigate without at least finding out what the local police already know and find out what leads, if any, they're currently pursuing."

"That's a good point, Steven," said Amanda. "Here are my thoughts. Almost any police department would be skeptical to work with someone from the outside. We need the upper hand. We need to give them information they don't already have. Now, as far as we know, they don't even know this is a copycat yet. They might, but if so, they've been tightlipped about it."

"So how do we get the upper hand?" asked Steven.

"Let's visit the crime scenes and find something, anything, that the investigators have missed," said Amanda.

"Perfect," said Doyle. "Here's what I think. William and I will head to western North Dakota and investigate two of the crime scenes. There was one just east of Dickinson and another south of Minot. That'll bring me near my dad's old stomping grounds. I wouldn't mind visiting the town of Garrison again."

"Remember what we'd discussed," said Amanda.

"Absolutely," said Doyle. "We'll only be tracking down this serial killer. I'm now completely hands-off the Unlucky Larry case."

Amanda nodded. "Good. I just don't want any trouble."

"Speaking of which," said Doyle. "Hanratty, I'd like you to stay with Amanda and Steven."

"What? Why?" asked Hanratty. "I mean, no offense." He lowered his eyes and looked away from Amanda.

"The crime scenes in eastern North Dakota are the freshest. I want your camera to capture everything. Even though I completely trust Amanda and Steven's skills, I'm an overly protective boyfriend who would like an extra set of hands to protect my damsel from any form of distress."

Amanda glared. "Call me a damsel again and I'll crush your nuts."

"Like I said—I completely trust your skills," said Doyle. "I'm just paranoid. Particularly when a serial killer is involved. Hopefully you can understand that."

"I do," said Amanda. "But I'll be fine."

"Let's all stay in communication," said Doyle. "Cell phones on at all times. The more info we relay to each other, the better. Remember— we have a chance at preventing more lives from being taken by this guy. Possibly many more lives."

Everyone around the table nodded.

"So Amanda, Steven, and Hanratty—you'll be heading to Grand Forks first, and then Devil's Lake right after. That was the most recent murder. They might even still have the crime scene tape up. Go see what's happening. And if you make contact with the police, let me know how it goes."

"Sounds good," said Amanda.

A six-foot-four space alien walked around the corner, carrying their tab.

"Could I interest you folks in any Martian Malts or Comet Cake?"

"How do you live with yourself, sir?" asked William.

"Excuse me?" asked the befuddled alien.

"Just give me that," said William, taking the tab. "Do you accept terrestrial credit cards, or do I need to do some form of currency exchange at an intergalactic bank?"

The alien removed the top half of his costume, revealing a much shorter college-aged kid with three days' worth of stubble on his cheeks.

"Listen, man—I make ten bucks an hour to wear this furnace of a costume and take people's abuse all day. Just pay your damn bill." He put the top of the costume back on, took William's credit card, and said, "Happy travels."

15

So where are we going first, Doyle?" asked William, simultaneously looking at a map of North Dakota while glancing at news articles on his laptop. "Dickinson, and then Minot?"

Doyle checked his gauge to make sure he wasn't speeding. "Yeah, let's check out the Dickinson crime scene first. We'll go to Minot afterwards. Although we may have a couple pit stops in-between."

"Oh?" asked William. "You mean for dinner? Or do they call it supper out here?"

"Supper," said Doyle. "And lunch is called dinner."

"So we just had dinner at noon?" asked William. "Apparently this isn't all that different than the U.K. Drive a couple hundred miles and you're in another country. Figuratively, in this circumstance."

"Right. And in addition to supper, I thought we might drop in on Sanderson's daughters," said Doyle. He began whistling as though he'd said nothing of significance.

"Oh, Doyle," said William. "You know as well as I do what Amanda's feelings were on that. Do you really want to put your relationship in jeopardy?"

Doyle stopped whistling. "I'm not doing anything of the sort. We're just going to ask a few questions. We won't solicit our services. We'll simply find out how Unlucky Larry's murder relates to the current string of Friendly Companion murders. And you know there's a connection—don't deny that."

"I certainly think there is. I'm just more concerned for you. Why do you want to approach this serial killer situation from that direction? Is it because of your father?"

"Yes," said Doyle. "It's obvious that this copycat isn't the same guy my dad arrested. But that doesn't mean my dad didn't overlook something. Maybe Dillman had a partner all along. It's possible."

"But unlikely. Serial killers generally don't go underground for twenty-five years. It's happened before, but . . ."

"If we can take a closer look at the original Friendly Companion, just maybe that'll shed some light on the copycat. It might help us track him down faster."

"You might be right, Doyle. I think it's worth a shot. However, I do not want you to expect me to lie to the others just to protect you and your relationship with Amanda. I don't care for drama, Doyle. This isn't *Maury*, for God's sake."

"You watch a lot of television during the day, don't you?"

"Only when I'm researching. I need something on in the background," said William. "Besides, one can learn so much about the American culture just by watching lots of television. For example, *Maury* has taught me that Americans are, by and large, truly terrible people."

"You need to watch some other shows," said Doyle. "Something that'll give you a better take on our culture."

"Like what?"

Thinking about it, Doyle said, "I have no idea."

Doyle adjusted the knob on the radio, trying to find a station that wasn't solely country music.

"Getting back to the task at hand," said Doyle. "What's up with this copycat? How many has he killed so far?"

"From what I can tell, there have been five so far," said William. "Based on the dates in these articles, it looks like Dickinson was first. That was roughly four months ago. Minot was the next. About two months ago. Then at the beginning of this month was the Bismarck murder, and then just two weeks ago was the Grand Forks murder. It's been less than a week since the Devil's Lake killing."

"Does that mean he's accelerating?"

"Unless we've missed a murder or two, yes, I believe it does."

"That's not good," said Doyle. "He could be killing someone right now and we wouldn't even know it."

"True, Doyle. That's why urgency is the name of the game. We'll have to figure this out as quickly as we can."

"I didn't put Amanda in harm's way, did I? By having her investigate the most recent murders?"

"I don't think so," said William. "She'd be in more danger if she were a small town resident with lots of her money in her house."

"Money," said Doyle. "Did the copycat murders have money stolen from their houses?"

"Not all of the articles make reference to that, but at least one of them does. In Bismarck, a safe was broken into and the contents were emptied. The police weren't certain what the contents were."

"Maybe that's the connection. How did Dillman know which homes would have lots of money? How does the copycat know?"

"That's a good question, Doyle. We'll have to see if the victims had a particular bank in common. That could be the connection."

"We won't know until we can start asking people some questions. How much further to Dickinson?" asked Doyle.

"We're still a couple hundred miles out," said William, observing the map. He looked out of the window. "There's certainly plenty of farmland in this state."

"Boy, is that an understatement," said Doyle. "Can we switch places? I think I'll take a nap."

16

"We're just coming into Grand Forks," said Steven. "Great," said Hanratty, lying down in the back of the car. "Let me know when we're leaving Grand Forks."

"You keep that up, you'll be staying in Grand Forks," said Amanda. "Get your camera equipment ready. Let's document everything."

"Would you like some picturesque panoramas of wheat fields? I can do that right now if you want."

"That's okay," said Amanda. "Just stick to the crime scenes for now."

"You got it."

"Did William e-mail you directions?" asked Steven.

"Yes," said Amanda. "Take the next exit, then take a right. We should pass a gas station, a grocery store, a small residential area, and a park. We're going to a farmhouse about five miles past all of that."

"Sounds good," said Steven. "So what's William's deal anyway?"

"His deal?" asked Amanda. "Well, he's straight, if that's what you mean."

"I figured that," said Steven. "Too bad, though. I love the British accent. But what's his story?"

"He used to investigate serial killers for Scotland Yard," said Amanda. "Like Wisconsin, London has more than its fair share, so he stayed quite busy. Then his wife, Eva, moved to Minnesota to pursue acting. Without William, that is."

"Ahh, they broke up," said Steven.

Amanda nodded. "He tracked her down. He was hoping to rekindle what had been lost. No such luck, though. I'd never seen a couple fight so violently before. And it certainly wasn't one-sided. They're both very strong, capable people."

"So, what happened?"

"After her last acting gig went sour, she moved back to London. Without William, again. This time, he didn't bother chasing after her. Now it's just Doyle and William. BFFs."

"Nice," said Steven. "So I just stay on this road?"

"Yes, the farmhouse should be straight ahead, another mile or two."

Steven decelerated, observing the thirty-mile-per-hour speed limit sign. "How are things between you and Doyle?"

Amanda shrugged. "Not bad. We've been through a lot, and we're still together. It's a good sign. I still feel like he has a lot to learn in the relationship department, but lucky for him, I'm fairly patient."

"He does have sort of a boyish charm about him," said Steven.

Hanratty made an audible gagging sound in the backseat.

"Don't get any ideas, Steven. He's mine," said Amanda.

"Not to worry. I won't try to take your man. But do you know how hard it is to find another man in uniform like me? Not so easy."

"I'm sure they're out there," said Amanda. "You just have to keep looking."

"I guess," said Steven. "I just don't want to date any more coffee baristas. All they do is bitch about customers. Boooring."

Amanda laughed. "I can imagine."

"Is that the farmhouse?" asked Steven. It was a small farmhouse, but kept up nicely. The white paint looked new, probably painted within the past year.

Amanda saw a mailbox on the side of the road that said "Gunderson." Amanda recognized the name from William's discussion at Space Aliens. "Yes, turn! Turn!" yelled Amanda.

As they approached, Amanda could see that there was still crime scene tape stretched across the doorway.

"I'm sure the local police won't mind if we just mosey on in and take some photos," said Hanratty. "Maybe play around with some things. Add a few extra fingerprints. They love when that happens."

"You've gotten sarcastic since you became unemployed," said Amanda.

"And I've been sober since ten o'clock. That makes for a pretty rough day," said Hanratty.

"Stop worrying and stop complaining. We'll have you take some photos, but we'll be very careful with everything. We just want to see if the local police missed anything during their investigation."

"Such as the jar of pickles that William saw in the newspaper article," said Steven.

"Exactly," said Amanda. "See—Steven knows how to be a team player."

"Yeah, yeah," said Hanratty.

Steven parked near the door of the farmhouse.

"Are we ready?" asked Steven.

Hanratty grabbed his camera bag. "Yup, let's do this."

As they walked towards the front stoop, Amanda saw a multitude of tire tracks on the dirt driveway.

"I wonder if the police tried to narrow down the assailant's tire tracks before mucking up the trail with their own."

"Good question," said Steven. "It's an easy enough mistake to make. I'll be honest, I wasn't thinking about that myself when I drove in."

Hanratty took snapshots of all the tire tracks. "I doubt this will be any use. But just in case," he said, as he continued to press buttons and adjust the lens.

Amanda removed the crime scene tape from the doorway and they walked inside.

"It's drafty in here," said Steven. "Really adds to the ambience."

"Agreed," said Amanda. She wished she'd worn a hooded sweatshirt rather than a t-shirt and vest.

Amanda guessed the farmhouse was maybe 1,200 square feet. The kitchen and dining area were immediately to the right of the entrance.

"Hanratty, take a photo of the pantry. The jar of pickles is still sitting there."

Hanratty took the shot. "Since the police weren't aware of it, I'm guessing they didn't dust the jar for prints."

"True," said Amanda. "But I highly doubt this copycat would be dumb enough to leave his prints everywhere."

"Unless he wants to get caught," said Hanratty.

"He's been clever enough up until this point," said Amanda. "I don't think it would do us any good."

"Look at this," said Steven. He was in the middle of a hallway leading from the kitchen to the living room. He was pointing at something.

At first, Amanda couldn't make out what it was. It was too dark in the room. Then she saw it. Blood stains.

Hanratty took several snapshots in a row from various vantage points. Amanda's eyes were going wonky from the constant flashes.

"That's a lot of blood," said Amanda. It just wasn't a single splotch, but several. Some had landed on a nearby wall.

"If I understand what William had said about the original Friendly Companion, then this new guy is using a different M.O.," said Steven. "Didn't the first guy just make the old ladies eat his poisoned pickles?"

"That's what I understand," said Amanda. "I'm calling Doyle."

She pulled out her cell phone and dialed.

"Hi, sweetie," said the voice on the other line.

"Hi, Doyle. Hey, please ask William if the Grand Forks article mentioned anything about the way Ms. Gunderson died."

She could hear Doyle talk to William.

"Nope, nothing," said Doyle. "It just said that she'd died of unnatural causes and that foul play was suspected. Why?"

"There's a lot of blood here," said Amanda.

"Oh," said Doyle. "That's not good."

Amanda could hear William in the background ask, "What's wrong?"

"Blood," said Doyle. "Lots of it."

Amanda heard William grunt.

"You know what this means? This guy is different. More violent," said Amanda.

Doyle sighed. "Be careful. I don't like the idea of a violent serial killer on the loose. Especially when you're at the most recent crime scene."

"I'll be fine," said Amanda. "Besides, I have Hanratty here to protect me."

Hanratty stuck out his tongue. Amanda heard more chatter on the phone.

"What's going on?" asked Amanda.

"William wants to know if you've found a safe yet," said Doyle. "Or any sign of theft. Dillman was known for taking money from his victims, and the copycat might be doing the same."

"Okay, I'll look. I'll give you a call later, okay?"

"You bet," said Doyle.

Amanda flipped her cell phone shut. "Okay, guys. Let's look for a broken safe, an empty shoebox, anything that looks like theft."

They dispersed through the house. Steven called, "Hey, look in here!"

Amanda and Hanratty followed down the short hallway to a quaint master bedroom. The room had been ransacked. Dresser drawers were pulled out, the bed mattress was crooked on the frame, boxes had been overturned in the closet.

"I don't know how we can determine if he found any money," said Steven. "But clearly he was looking for something."

"Hanratty, can you take photos of absolutely everything?" asked Amanda.

"Sure, why not."

"Steven, let's check out the rest of the house," said Amanda.

"What are we looking for?" asked Steven.

Amanda thought about it. "I guess I'd just like some idea of his plans. Where is he going next? How is he choosing his victims? There could be clues in this house. We just need to find them."

"That sounds like a needle in a haystack," said Steven. "But, what the heck. Let's have a looksee."

17

Doyle," said William, looking in the rear view mirror. "Doyle?" He threw a half-eaten bagel at Doyle's face. Doyle awoke immediately from his nap in the backseat. Cream cheese was smeared across his nose.

"What? What is it? Are we under attack? Am I hit?" Doyle's eyes bounced around the scenery outside. "Oh, we're in North Dakota."

"Did you think you were back in Vietnam? Wait, you're not old enough for that. Iraq?" asked William.

"I've never been a soldier," said Doyle. "I've played a lot of *Call of Duty*, though."

"I see," said William. "I just wanted to make you aware that we're nearing the scene of the first copycat murder. You may want to wake up."

"Yup, yup. I'm up. What have I missed?"

"Look around you," said William. "Not a bloody thing."

Doyle looked at his cell phone. "Ahh, hell. I've missed a bunch of texts."

"Anything important?" asked William.

"They're all from Amanda," said Doyle. "Nothing too important. Just wondering why I wasn't responding."

"I'm sure she assumed you were sleeping," said William.

"That's probably why she sent a text that said, '*You're not sleeping again, are you?*'"

William chuckled. Doyle was the sort of man who wasn't terribly difficult to figure out.

"Nothing else, though? She's not in grave danger?"

"It doesn't appear so," said Doyle. "Except for this. *'Found bank statements. Grand Forks victim withdrew $50k from Garrison Bank 6 months ago.*"

"That's where Larry Sanderson was from," said William. "And where his wife was murdered."

"That's also where one of his daughters lives, right?"

"It is," said William.

"Let's skip this murder scene, then. Let's go straight to Garrison."

William shook his head. "We'll go there right shortly. But we have to investigate this crime scene first. Let's see if we can find bank statements at the victim's house. If there's the same connection, then we'll have evidence for the authorities."

"Authorities? Please. We won't have to worry about them until we deliver this killer to them in handcuffs."

"It'll be that easy, eh, Doyle?"

"Of course," said Doyle. "We're professionals, after all." Doyle wiped his nose, and hand came away smeared in cream cheese. "What the—"

"What was that you saying about professionals?" asked William, smiling.

"Grow up, William," said Doyle. "This is no time for your British Benny Hill-type shenanigans."

"Whatever you say."

* * *

"This is the house?" asked Doyle.

"This is it," said William. "Ms. Caroline Reyes. She was killed months ago, but hopefully we can still find some useful clues."

Doyle looked around. "This is more populated than I thought it would be," said Doyle. They were in a residential area just east of Dickinson. It wasn't too different than some of the outer suburbs of the Twin Cities. "If she screamed, that could have alerted the neighbors for sure."

"That's a good point, Doyle. We still have to pinpoint his reasons for choosing his particular victims. Maybe he wasn't pleased by the location, either."

They walked up to the door. There was no longer any crime scene tape. Doyle wasn't surprised since it had been months since Caroline Reyes had been murdered. Doyle walked into a small flowerbed underneath a front window, grabbed ahold of a ledge, and pulled himself up to look inside the window.

"This place has to be vacant," said Doyle.

"What do you see?"

"A whole lot of nothing," said Doyle. "This room should be the kitchen, but no refrigerator, no microwave, no toaster. It looks like this place has been cleaned out."

"By now the family has probably come through and collected the belongings they wanted," said William. "This could make our job a little more complicated."

"We might still be able to find something," said Doyle. He knocked on the door, knowing full well he wouldn't get a response from anyone inside. He tried turning the doorknob, but it was locked.

"This is okay," said William. "I'll simply call the local police station and ask if they wouldn't mind cooperating with us during this investigation. Certainly an unsolved murder would be a top priority for them, and I have no doubt that—"

An audible slam tore William from his train of thought. Doyle had launched himself into the locked door.

"Doyle, really, I don't think this is an appropriate—"

Doyle jolted his body into the door again, this time causing a loud cracking sound as the wood of the door gave way along with the hinges. Doyle fell on top of the door as it crashed to the ground.

William looked around, happily confirming that no one in the immediate vicinity had seen, and hopefully not heard, a thing.

"That's one way of doing it," said William.

"I'm pretty strong."

"I wouldn't have thought it, but I suppose you're right."

"All right, let's look around," said Doyle. He held up his hand, and William grabbed it and boosted him off the rubble on the floor. As Doyle brushed off his legs, he saw something that took him aback.

"I'm not bleeding am I?" asked Doyle, touching all his vital areas—neck, wrists . . . genitals.

"No, Doyle. That's not your blood. It's been there a long time."

Blood had been sprayed across the lower part of the wall in the main entrance and had continued in a smeared trail along the carpet.

"What happened here, William? Did he shoot her? Just like that? Or was she stabbed?"

"Help me lift this door," said William. Doyle and William picked up the door then moved it to the side, leaning it against the wall.

Underneath the door was more blood. William brushed his hand across the carpet. "Here. A bullet hole."

"In the carpet?" asked Doyle. "Does that mean he shot her execution style?"

"Maybe. But I don't think so. He may've shot her leg to stop her from running or fighting, then dragged her down the hall. Remember, Doyle—he's a serial killer. He doesn't want her dead too quick."

"That's sick."

"Yes, it is," said William. "I've dealt with some of the sickest in England for many years. Humans are capable of some pretty terrible things."

"How did you deal with all of that?"

"Not very well. I brought many very bad people into custody, but I also became a severe alcoholic and a borderline lunatic in the process. It's hard to not let some of these creeps into your head."

"Wait," said Doyle. "If he shot her in the leg, wouldn't she scream? There are too many houses around here. Someone could have heard her."

"Maybe. But if so, the local police are probably aware of that. I don't think we need be concerned. Besides, I'm guessing if she screamed, it was brief."

"Why do you say that?"

"I'm sure he was on her fast. He probably either strangled her, or at least brought a knife to her neck."

"Oh, God—you think he sliced her neck open?"

William shook his head. "No, I don't think so. We'd see a lot more spatter if that was the case."

Doyle was silent.

"But I think we should start looking in the rooms and find out—"

William heard a groan. He turned his head to see Doyle running out the front door and losing his lunch on what had once been a lovely, fragrant flowerbed.

William approached Doyle. "Are you okay?"

Doyle held up his hand. "Hold on." He heaved again.

"Listen, if this is too much for you, it's fine to wait in the car."

"No, no, I'm all right," said Doyle. "It must be that greasy Space Aliens food. I should avoid that in the future."

"So it had nothing to do with all the blood in the hallway?"

Doyle groaned again.

"Just kidding, Doyle. Why don't you stay out here for a few minutes. I'm going to do a little snooping around."

* * *

Doyle sat in the passenger seat of William's car. He chewed on some Wintergreen Altoids. He took out his cell phone and called Amanda.

"You're awake!" said Amanda.

"Yeah, I'm awake," said Doyle. "What are you up to?"

"Heading towards the crime scene in Devil's Lake. We'll see what clues we can gather there. Any luck in Dickinson?"

"Well, I've done some pretty good investigating. Uncovered some clues. Analyzed the crime scene."

"I'm surprised you're doing so well," said Amanda. "Usually if there's any blood around, you don't do so hot."

"I have no idea what you're talking about," said Doyle. He put another Altoid into his mouth. "How are things with Steven and Hanratty?"

Amanda didn't respond.

"Honey?" asked Doyle

"Fine," said Amanda.

Oh, shit, thought Doyle. *That's always bad.* "Is everything okay with Steven?"

"Yes, Steven is doing a terrific job."

"How about Hanratty?"

"Well, you keep up that investigating, Doyle. We'll talk later."

Terrific, thought Doyle. "Let me know if you uncover anything interesting in Devil's Lake. We're heading towards Garrison next."

"Remember what we talked about, Doyle. Don't question anyone about Unlucky Larry's murder. We're not looking into that case."

"I know, I know," said Doyle. "You have my word."

Doyle hung up. As if right on queue, William stormed out of Caroline Reyes's residence with paperwork in his hands.

William got into the driver's seat. "Bank statements," he said, holding them up.

"Which bank?"

"Guess," said William.

"So that's it, then," said Doyle. "The killer got his information from Garrison Bank. How much was this withdrawal?"

"Eighty thousand dollars."

"Why are all these old folks taking out their life savings?"

"That's a great question," said William. "Maybe they're being coerced to do so. Or maybe they just don't trust the banks. The economy hasn't exactly been steady lately, has it?"

"That's true," said Doyle. "But still—that's so much money."

"Keeping money in a shoebox is safer than keeping it in a spiraling stock market," said William, starting the car. "Do you suppose we should alert the authorities about a break-in?"

"Nah," said Doyle, observing the vacant doorway. "Someone will see it and give them a call."

"Your sense of responsibility never ceases to amaze me," said William.

"No need to compliment me. I already know I'm fantastic."

"Okay," said William. "Let's go to Garrison."

18

"Doyle, open my laptop," said William, not taking his eyes off the road.

"You got it. What am I doing with this?"

"Look up the Garrison Bank. See if they have an online staff directory. Our assumption at this point has to be that either the Friendly Companion works there or he knows someone who does. I'm curious who our suspect pool might include."

"Good idea."

"What do you see?"

"Hold on, hold on," said Doyle. "I'm not used to using a computer for things other than looking at naked ladies."

"Heaven's sake. Let me know when you have something."

"Here we are! Yes, there's a listing of all the employees."

"Well, who's on it?" Doyle could hear the impatience in his voice.

"Let's see here. Gus Davidson is the bank president. Keith Markt is the vice-president. Stephanie Hullman is a teller. Hmm. Wait a minute."

"What? What is it?"

"You're not going to believe this."

"Good God, Doyle, you're killing me. What is it?"

"Mae Sanderson. Unlucky Larry's daughter. She's a bank teller."

"Oh, my," said William. "Oh, my."

"I think we've found a string that connects the Friendly Companion to Unlucky Larry's murder," said Doyle.

"Yes, but now we need to know the nature of that string. How does Mae Sanderson know the Friendly Companion?"

"Or is *she* the Friendly Companion?"

"I guess we have to be open to that possibility," said William. "But my gut tells me no. It's probably more complicated than that. Especially considering her mother was killed by the Friendly Companion, or the original one, I should say. That's not to say she couldn't be a really twisted individual."

"I can't wait to talk to her. This is going to be exciting."

"Doyle, look up the bank hours on the website."

"Let's see . . . standard bank hours. Nine to five."

"It's four o'clock right now."

"We gotta be a good ninety miles out still, right?" asked Doyle.

"Yes, indeed." William's foot pressed down on the accelerator. Hard.

"Really, William? I didn't think you had it in you," said Doyle, watching the needle on the speedometer rise. "You're a speed demon."

"What do you Minnesotans like to say so much?" asked William. "You betcha?"

"Funny." Doyle swallowed. He hoped he wouldn't have to worry about a reappearance of Space Aliens fine cuisine.

* * *

William pulled onto the frontage road, took a right after the Garrison Motel, took a left to hit Main Street, then proceeded towards the bank.

"The online town map is helpful, but I bet we couldn't drive five minutes in Garrison without running into the bank. There's not a whole heck of a lot here."

"Except for that," said William, pointing at the giant metal fish. "What in God's name is that?"

"That's Wally the Walleye. The town's pride. He protects the town's fishing museum."

"I see," said William.

"It's been several years since I've been back here. That was for my dad's funeral."

"I'm sorry," said William.

"No, it's okay. It was actually a bizarre experience. His funeral happened to take place during the town's annual Dickens Festival. The entire town gets decorated like nineteenth-century England. I never thought I'd have to go see my father at Ye Olde Funeral Home."

William laughed. "I'm sure that brought some light to an otherwise dark situation."

"It did," said Doyle. "I've never been a fan of the incredibly long drive to get here, but once you're here, it's not so bad."

William nodded. "So the bank is right at the end of Main Street? Is that right?"

"You got it."

William pulled into a parking spot.

"William, the bank is still another half block down that way."

"I know," said William. "The employees should be leaving in the next five minutes. Let's watch for Mae Sanderson."

"How do we know what she looks like?"

"How many employees were on the online directory?"

"Six," said Doyle.

"How many were women?"

"Two."

"I think we'll figure it out," said William.

Doyle took a drink of Diet Coke from a bottle he'd been nursing. "This is exciting," he said. "Like covert ops stuff."

William glanced at the giant fish again and said, "Yes, that's exactly what this is like."

Doyle nearly slugged William in the shoulder. "Is that her?"

The woman who exited the bank was a hefty woman, not necessarily fat, but she had a large structure. Her eyes darted back and forth. Doyle realized she carried herself in the same manner that Unlucky Larry had. It had to be his daughter.

"Let's get her—" Doyle said, but William was already out of the car. "Hey, wait up."

William had already confronted the potential Mae when Doyle caught up.

"—sorry, Ms. Sanderson," William was saying, "but we really need to talk to you."

"What is this about?" asked the woman. When she saw Doyle, her eyes grew wide and she fell to the ground.

"Ms. Sanderson?" William asked, reaching down to help her up.

She looked scared to death of Doyle.

"You're dead," said the woman.

"Hey, this is no time for threats," said Doyle.

The woman blinked, gathered her wits, and grabbed ahold of William's hand, who pulled her onto her feet. Doyle realized it must have taken some strength on William's part, because he was flexing and unflexing his arm afterward.

"Are you Mae Sanderson?" asked Doyle. He saw the woman exhale. She swallowed hard.

"Yes, yes I am. Sorry—I thought you were someone else. You look exactly like a cop I used to know. But he's . . . not around anymore."

Doyle assumed he knew who she was talking about. He was incredibly curious how she knew his dad, but he didn't want to tip his hand quite yet. Doyle looked at William, and his eyes were telling him the same thing.

"Mae, can we go somewhere and talk?"

Mae Sanderson eyed both of them nervously.

"I already know what happened to my dad. My sister Clara called me last night. You can save your breath."

"Actually," said William, his face pulling taut and rigid. To Doyle, he looked intimidating. Serious. It was a good act. "We'd like to talk to you about something else."

"I don't have anything I want to talk about," said Mae. "Now if you'll excuse me."

"I'd think you'd want to help us," said William. "Lives are at stake."

Mae considered her options. "Fine. I knew this day would come eventually. If you want me to talk, I need my lawyer present. And I want to be guaranteed complete protection and immunity."

Doyle looked at William, who nodded back at him. "Ms. Sanderson, I'm sorry if we gave you the wrong impression. We're not cops."

"You're not? Then who are you? What do you want with me?" Doyle thought she was on the verge of screaming for help.

"We're private detectives," Doyle blurted out. "We're trying to figure out who killed your father."

Mae Sanderson seemed to relax instantly. William smiled at Doyle. *That was the right thing to say*, his expression suggested.

"Okay," said Mae. "I'll help however I can. I don't know how much help I'll be, though."

"Let's go somewhere more private," said William. "That giant fish is making me uncomfortable."

19

The Friendly Companion sat in his car, watching in disbelief. Who were these people?

He'd come back to Mildred Stanton's house in Devil's Lake, hoping to take care of some unfinished business. Namely the hundred grand that he should have been able to find in her house but was unable to.

He figured enough time had passed where the police would have cleared out, and if anyone questioned him going to the house, they'd certainly realize he was just a poor, uninformed salesman who had an appointment to discuss insurance matters with Ms. Stanton. Not that she would need it anymore, of course.

That's why he came during the day. Someone goes into the house of a murdered woman in the evening, then something downright suspicious is happening. In the middle of the day, it's simply a misunderstanding.

Everything would have worked out perfectly, if it weren't for the inexplicable appearance of a Honda Accord in the driveway. It had Minnesota plates. If they were cops, they were certainly out of their jurisdiction.

A skinny guy came out of the house and went into the car. He pulled out a black bag with a strap. Jesus, was that a camera bag? What were they doing in there?

After not too long, a slick looking bastard walked out and stretched his arms. He looked a little too chiseled. That would be unusual for a cop. They were usually flabby from all the time spent in a patrol car and completing paperwork. He still wasn't sure what kind of people he was dealing with.

Then he saw her. Flowing blonde hair. Tight jeans. A t-shirt that clung to her well-proportioned body. Her ass looked unbelievable. She reminded him of his wife when she was young. Not all old and saggy.

He felt a stirring in his underpants, then bit his lip from the pain. Some unexpected shifting had caused a scab to tear off. So soon after it'd healed from all that scratching . . .

He tried to focus. The woman—she had to be a reporter. That was the only way to explain her beauty. That, combined with the thin man with the camera, it all made sense. They were putting a story together. About the Friendly Companion? Probably not. He didn't think they'd figured that out quite yet. He hadn't heard anything about the Valley City murder yet. That was the bomb just waiting to go off.

He wanted that reporter. In more ways than one. He wanted to tell her all about his exploits. The things he'd done. The things he'd continue to do. He might even show her a few things.

But he didn't want to be impulsive. That'd gotten him into trouble before. He had to be patient. He'd keep an eye on her. Maybe watch where she went tonight.

He hadn't felt this excited in a long time. Heck, not since his first murder.

Normally he wasn't one to mix business and pleasure. But for this woman . . . he might make an exception.

He rubbed his pants, trying to soothe his aching genitals. *Pickle juice*, he thought. *The bane of my existence.*

The thin man put a camera into the bag, then threw it in the backseat. The young, strong-looking guy climbed into the passenger seat. The unbelievable blonde was busy pushing buttons on her cell phone. Probably texting. That's what all the young women did nowadays. After a few seconds she stopped texting, put the phone in her jacket pocket, and climbed into the driver's seat of the Accord.

As the vehicle pulled out of the driveway, the Friendly Companion lowered his head. He was parked on the side of the road. He hoped they'd pass right by without noticing.

Sure enough, he heard the car go by. He looked up in time to see the taillights. He turned the key in his ignition, flipped a U-turn, and followed the Accord from a safe distance.

He didn't know where she was headed tonight, but he'd find out. He'd be there.

The killer smiled.

20

Mae Sanderson's hand shook, almost spilling the cheap black coffee that the Garrison Public Library provided to its patrons free of charge. They sat in a small conference room in the library not much bigger than a Volkswagen. Doyle concluded that conferences in Garrison usually didn't include more than a couple people.

For Doyle, the room reminded him of being in an interrogation room back in Minneapolis. It'd been a few years since he had the pleasure of weaseling his way into the mind of a suspect to get the information he needed. However, Doyle decided he'd better be gentle with Mae. He got the distinct impression the slightest disturbance could cause her to bolt out the door.

Doyle took a sip from the Styrofoam cup in his hand. He winced at the flavor. It tasted nothing like the coffee at the Rabbit Hole back in Minneapolis.

"Ms. Sanderson," said Doyle. "How much did your sister Clara tell you last night about your father's death?"

"That he'd been murdered. Shot in the chest. Several times," she said, casting her eyes downward.

Doyle realized now that she looked older than he initially thought. Her eyes were sunken. It looked like make-up covered what would otherwise be heavy wrinkles around her eyes. Doyle wondered how much of that was age and how much was from fear. Maybe a lifetime of it.

William added, "He was on stage. Whoever shot him was very bold, very cunning. Obviously he or she had little fear of being caught."

Doyle noticed Mae look up when William said *she*. He wondered if Mae was reading any implications into what William was saying.

"Do you know anyone who might want to kill your father?" asked William. "Any enemies?"

Mae shook her head. "No, he was liked by most people. He was really nice."

"Really nice," said William. "That's a rather weak description. When's the last time you saw your father?"

Mae looked uncomfortable. "It's been some years. We really weren't that close."

"What about your sisters?" asked Doyle. "How do you get along with them?"

"We don't," said Mae.

"But your sister called you last night," said Doyle. "You must be somewhat close."

"Trust me, we're not," said Mae. "Clara told me about Dad's death, and that's been the extent of our relationship in the last twenty years. Both of my sisters still blame me for our mother's death. That's never going to change."

"Why would they blame you for her death?" asked Doyle. "You didn't kill her, did you?"

Mae's eyes burned with rage. "I'm not saying anything more. Not without a lawyer present."

"Again, Mae—may I call you Mae? We're not cops," said William. "We're detectives attempting to find out who killed your father. We may not be able to do it without your help."

Mae squeezed her eyes shut and rubbed her temples. "I don't know who killed him."

"Did you see the newspaper that came out some weeks ago?" asked William. "The one that told about your father's death before it happened?"

Mae nodded. "I saw it."

"What did you make of that?" asked William.

"I thought maybe it was true. I called my sister Tabby in Minot. She wasn't happy to hear from me. She called Clara, and then spoke to Dad on the phone. Tabby called me back when she found out it was a hoax. She waited a couple days, though. Isn't that nice?"

"Who would write an article like that? Why?" asked Doyle.

"It was a message, maybe? Someone dredging up old business?" Mae fidgeted with a button on her blouse.

"What does that mean?" asked Doyle.

"I don't know."

"That's not helping us too much," said William.

"I don't know what else to say."

"You said your sisters blamed you for your mother's death. A man went to prison for her death. What do you know of the Friendly Companion killer?" asked William.

"He's dead," said Mae. "I'm not sure there's much else to say about him."

"How did you know him?" asked William.

"What do you mean?"

William got off his chair and knelt down on one knee next to Mae. Doyle was impressed by the move.

"Ms. Sanderson," said William. "Your sisters blamed you. You said so yourself. They wouldn't blame you unless you had some connection to her killer. So what was the connection? How did you know Fred Dillman?"

When Dillman's name was mentioned, Mae Sanderson looked up from her fidgeting hands. Her eyes welled up.

"He used me," she said.

Doyle and William exchanged glances.

"Could you explain further?" asked William.

The floodgates opened. Doyle saw years of pent-up sadness, grief, and regret pour out of Mae Sanderson. Maybe a little guilt? He wasn't sure yet.

"We dated. Back in 1985. I was only seventeen. A bank teller," she said, wiping her face with the sleeve of her blouse. "He was twenty-five and handsome. I also assumed he was rich. Who hadn't heard of Dillman's Kosher Dills? I had no idea the company was bankrupt. The pickles still sat on store shelves for years afterwards. I don't know if anyone knew the company went belly up."

William rubbed his chin. "He got information from you, didn't he? Bank customers' private information."

"I was young. I was dumb," she said. "I was naïve. I assumed he had more than enough money. I thought he was just being curious when he asked me all those questions."

"What specifically did he ask about?"

"Withdrawals," said Mae. "He wanted to know who was taking all their money out of the bank."

"That didn't raise any red flags with you?" asked Doyle.

She glared at him. "It seems obvious now, but he was a really smooth talker. I didn't know what he was doing."

"And your mother was one of the customers who made a withdrawal, wasn't she?" asked William.

Mae looked back down at her hands. "Yes. I'd told Freddy that my mom was thinking about leaving my dad. She was ready to do it. She withdrew all her money out of the bank."

"But she never got a chance to leave him," said Doyle.

"No. She was killed before she had a chance to pack. I was the one who found her. It was terrible. There was pickle juice everywhere."

"When did your sisters find out that it was you who supplied the financial information to Fred Dillman?" asked William.

"I don't think they ever figured out that much. They knew the man I'd dated killed our mom. That was enough for them to hate me for the rest of my life."

William studied her. "Ms. Sanderson, I find it hard to believe that, with all of the victims having major withdrawals coming from the same bank, the police didn't piece together that you were the source. That would have made big news. Your sisters would have heard about that."

"The police knew," said Mae. "At least, the lead investigator did." She looked at Doyle. "You're related, aren't you? Harry Malloy. He must have been your uncle? Your dad, maybe?"

"My dad," said Doyle, suddenly feeling that there were too many ghosts involved with this case. "He knew? That you'd given the information to Dillman?"

"Sure," said Mae. "He knew. Shortly after Freddy killed my mom, I was completely distraught. Destroyed. I tried killing myself."

"What did you do?" asked Doyle.

"I climbed all the way to the top of the fish statue and jumped off," said Mae.

"That wouldn't kill you."

"I know," said Mae. "I found that out pretty quickly. I broke two ribs and my left arm. Harry Malloy visited me when I was in the hospital. I told him everything. I knew at that point that it didn't matter. My life would never be the same."

"Ms. Sanderson, when is the last time you gave out confidential client information?" asked William.

"Not since I was seventeen. I was lucky to keep my job. Fortunately I'd gone to school with the bank president's daughter, so they knew me pretty well. Why, was there an identity theft of some sort?"

"No," said William. "But you're positive you haven't given out any information?"

"Definitely not," said Mae. "Please, I learned my lesson years ago. I'll never be that naïve again."

"Who else works at the bank?" asked William. "Women, specifically."

"Just me," said Mae. "And the new girl, Steph."

William glanced at Doyle, and Doyle responded with a nod.

"What's going on here? Why are you asking all these questions? This isn't just about my dad, is it?"

"I'm afraid not," said William.

"A copycat killer is following the same methods as Fred Dillman," said Doyle. "We thought maybe you were feeding the information to the copycat. But now it seems we need to talk to Steph. Where can we find her?"

"She usually walks home," said Mae. "She's probably there by now."

"Can you show us?" asked William.

"Yeah, I drove her home once when it was raining out. I'm pretty sure I remember which house was hers."

"Let's go," said Doyle. "We don't have any time to lose."

21

Can we eat?" asked Hanratty. "I'm hungry."

"You've been saying that for two hours," said Amanda.

"I've been hungry for two hours."

"We'll stop soon," said Amanda.

Steven, who took over driving duties after they stopped for gas, asked, "Is that car following us?"

Amanda looked in the side-view mirror. "I don't think so."

"Oh, please," said Hanratty. "There are no other cars on the road. You see one, suddenly you think you're being followed. If there were even one more car on the road, you wouldn't think anything of it."

"It's just . . . I'm pretty sure it's been the same car since we left Grand Forks. We're not exactly taking the most direct route."

"Just a coincidence," said Hanratty. "Steven, you're being paranoid."

"But he stopped at the gas station, too. For the same length of time we did."

"Cars need gas," said Hanratty. "And most vehicles take about the same amount of time to fill."

"Let's just pull into the next restaurant," said Amanda. "We'll see if he follows us."

Five minutes later, they came across a gas station that had a connected Taco John's.

"Really? This counts as a restaurant?" asked Hanratty.

"Shush," said Amanda.

"Even a stalker isn't self-destructive enough to eat at Taco John's."

"We're just going to see if he follows us," said Amanda.

As they pulled into the parking lot, the car behind them continued down the highway, not slowing down a bit.

"See?" said Hanratty. "Now can we go somewhere where we can actually eat?"

22

"Your dad was a really great guy," said Mae Sanderson from the backseat of William's car. "He was understanding. He was completely focused on catching Freddy."

"He might not have if it weren't for the old lady. What was her name?" asked Doyle.

"Edna Myrtle," said Mae. "Knocked him over the head with a rolling pin. Like something out of a Sunday-morning comic strip."

"She still around?" asked Doyle.

"I'm not sure," said Mae. "She doesn't have an account with us anymore. I guess that's no big surprise."

Doyle nodded. "How far are we from . . ." he checked his notes, ". . . Steph Hullman's house?"

"Should be just around the corner," said Mae. As William took a right, Mae pointed at a small white house with an overgrown driveway.

"This is an old house," said Doyle.

"I think she lives with her grandparents," said Mae. "I'm sure she'll be out of this town within a couple years. Teenagers don't last too long here."

"Not too many raves, I take it," said Doyle.

"What's a rave?" asked Mae.

"A party. But usually with techno music and illegal drugs."

"Oh," said Mae. "No, we don't have that here. Burt's Bar has music on the weekends, but it's usually country. Although they do have chewing tobacco there."

"That's close enough to a rave, I guess," said Doyle. He saw William roll his eyes.

"Here we are," said William, putting the car in park.

"I don't have to go with, do I?" asked Mae. "I mean, I don't want her to think I'm ratting her out."

"You can stay here," said William. "We'll come get you if we need you."

Doyle and William got out of the car and approached the house. Doyle pushed the doorbell button. It made a funny crackling sound and Doyle felt a jolt ride up through his arm. "Yow!" he yelled.

"What's wrong?" asked William.

"Just a little faulty wiring," said Doyle. He used the unzapped arm to knock on the door. Loudly. He wasn't in the mood for manners.

An old man with pants that rode up to his chest answered the door. He had a hearing aid the size of a nectarine in his ear.

"Who are you?" he asked with a strained voice.

"Sir, you have some seriously bad wiring here," said Doyle, pointing to the doorbell button.

"Brad who?"

"Bad wiring," repeated Doyle.

"Never heard of ya," said the old man. "And you?"

"William."

"Jillian? That's awfully feminine for a man, isn't it? Must be one of those L.A. types," said the old man, shaking his head.

"I'm from the U.K.," said William.

"No, I'm not gay," said the old man. "What is this? Who are you people?"

"We're here to see your granddaughter," said Doyle, speaking loudly. "Can we speak with her?"

"Depends. You're not a couple of those Internet perverts, are you? She's already got a boyfriend, you know."

"We didn't know that. Who's her boyfriend?" asked William.

The old man grunted. "Hugh's her boyfriend? I don't think so. I'm pretty sure his name's Eddie."

"We'll ask her ourselves," said William, putting his hand on the door, prepared to push it all the way open.

"Fine, come in," said the old man, slowly moving aside so Doyle and William could enter.

"Lovely home you have here, sir," said Doyle.

"Huh? What?"

"Lovely home," said Doyle, louder this time.

"Oh, bullshit. It's small and it smells like old people. Yes, I smell it, too. Too damn old and lazy to care anymore."

Doyle heard a noise from down the hall. A young red-haired girl emerged. "Grandpa, what's going on?"

"Couple perverts here to see you," said the old man.

"What?" she asked.

"We're detectives," said William. "Not perverts."

"Not entirely, anyway," said Doyle.

William shot him a look.

"Ms. Hullman, we're here to talk to you about your boyfriend," said William.

"How do you know about Eddie?" asked Stephanie. "Grandpa, what did you tell them?"

"Huh?"

Stephanie cupped her hands together and spoke directly into his hearing aid. "What did you tell them about Eddie?"

"Nothing. They figured it out themselves. They must be really good detectives."

"Actually, you told us, sir," said Doyle.

"Perverts *and* traitors. Terrific," said the old man.

"Can you give us some privacy, Grandpa?" asked Stephanie. "Let's go sit in the dining room." She motioned for Doyle and William to follow her.

"You have fun chatting about interwebs and eharmonies and whatever crap you kids talk about nowadays. I'll be in the living room watchin' my westerns."

"Thanks, Grandpa."

As he left the hallway for the living room, Stephanie directed Doyle and William to the small dining room adjacent to the kitchen. They sat down.

"Can I get you anything?" she asked.

"No, thank you," said William. "We really just want to ask you some questions."

"I'll have some pie," said Doyle.

William glared at Doyle, who shrugged it off. "It's North Dakota, William. Everyone has pie."

Stephanie cocked an eyebrow, but nodded in agreement. "Yeah, okay. Apple or cherry?"

"Apple would be great," said Doyle. "Thank you so much."

William shook his head at Doyle. "Why, Doyle? Why?"

"I like pie," said Doyle. "It's the best part about this state."

Doyle could see that Stephanie was also brewing a pot of coffee for them.

"What's this all about, Detectives?" she asked, as she grabbed three mugs out of a cupboard.

"Your boyfriend, Ms. Hullman," said William. "And all the bank information you've given to him."

Stephanie dropped a mug on the floor. It shattered into little pieces.

"I'm such a klutz sometimes," she said. "But seriously, I have no idea what you're talking about."

"We know you didn't mean to give him the information. He just pried it out of you little by little. Does that sound about right?"

"You're making Eddie sound like some sort of criminal master-mind," said Stephanie, laughing nervously. "I may have let a few things slip that I shouldn't have, but it was just casual conversation. He wouldn't do anything with it."

"He already has, Stephanie," said William.

She stopped picking pieces off the ground. Instead, she walked straight over to the dining room table, pulled out a chair, and sat down. "Please tell me what's going on."

"My pie—" Doyle began to say, but was cut off by William.

"First, Ms. Hullman, let me hear you describe your boyfriend," said William.

"By the way, please call me Steph. 'Ms. Hullman' sounds way too much like my grandmother."

"Fine, Steph," said William. "What does your boyfriend look like?"

"He's tall. Handsome. Brown hair, brown eyes. He's strong."

"How does he dress?"

"Really sophisticated like. He's in business school, so he has to."

"How old is he?"

"Early twenties," said Steph.

"Are you sure?" asked William.

She shrugged. "Maybe he's a bit older." She paused, and her cheeks took on color. "Maybe a lot older. He told me early twenties. I didn't press him on it."

"What's his full name?"

"Eddie? Well, it's Edward Dillberg. I don't know his middle name."

Doyle and William once again exchanged glances.

"Did you say Edward *Dillberg*?" asked William.

"Yeah? Why? Is he wanted or something?"

Doyle had all but forgotten about his pie. "Have you heard of Fred Dillman?"

"No," said Steph. "Familiar name, though. Is he related to Eddie?"

"Kinda," said Doyle. "Isn't that weird, William? What are the chances of a copycat having a name so similar to the original?"

Steph furrowed her brow. "Huh?"

William shook his head. "I have a feeling Edward Dillberg isn't his real name. He's toying with us."

"Oh," said Doyle. "Yeah, I guess that makes more sense."

"Not his real name? Toying? Copycat? What are you guys talking about?"

"Listen, Steph," said William. "We'll tell you everything later. For now, I need you to do one thing for me. Write down the names of all the bank customers you may have mentioned to Eddie. Can you do that?"

"Yeah, I think so. Am I in trouble?"

"Not necessarily. As long as you help us out, you might be fine. I can't promise anything, though," said William.

She nodded. "Okay. I'll find some paper."

"Feel free to get that pie, too," said Doyle, and William swiftly punched him in the arm.

Steph walked back into the room with a slice of pie, a Post-it note, and a pen. She placed the pie in front of Doyle, then sat down and began scribbling on the Post-it note.

"Be sure to include *all* the names," said William. "This is extremely important."

"I got it," said Steph.

"Take your time," said Doyle, with his mouth stuffed full of apples and cinnamon.

It didn't take her long. After a minute of writing, pausing, then writing again, she finally laid the pen down on the table and handed the note to William.

"How many names?" asked Doyle, crumbs falling from his lips.

"Six," said William. "And I recognize five of them from the articles."

"What does that mean?" asked Doyle.

"It means one woman is in very grave danger," said William.

"How so?" asked Steph.

"Like I said, we'll fill you in later. Nothing to worry about now," said William. "But do you happen to know where this Maddie Benson lives?"

"I don't see her too often," said Steph. "I think she lives way east. Valley City, maybe?"

"That's a long way from here," said Doyle. "That's practically on the Minnesota border."

"Amanda," said William. "And Steven and Hanratty. They'll be closest. Do you know where they are right now?"

"I think they were headed towards Bismarck," said Doyle. "But it shouldn't be too bad for them to double back and head toward Valley City."

"We need to call them right away," said William.

Doyle shoveled the remaining pie into his mouth. Whipped cream was smeared across his upper lip.

"Fanks for da pie," said Doyle. A few crumbs inadvertently flew out of his mouth and hit Steph Hullman in the face.

"You're welcome," said Steph. "Listen, I have no idea what Eddie's done. But whatever it is—take it easy on him, okay? He's a really sweet, sensitive guy."

"I'm sure he is," said Doyle. "I bet he's just misunderstood. Like the bad kid from *The Breakfast Club*."

"What's that? There's a club in town I wasn't invited to?"

"Oh, God," said Doyle. "Kids today."

"Just call me if anything happens to Eddie. I want to know what's going on."

"Don't worry. You'll be informed," said Doyle. William was already out the door by the time Doyle caught up to him.

After they exited, they heard an old man's voice yell, "And stay out!" This was followed by him saying, "Are we mad at them?" Then, much louder, "Never mind. Thanks for comin' out."

* * *

When Doyle and William left the house, they saw that Mae Sanderson was no longer in the backseat of the car. The rear passenger door stood wide open.

"Huh," said Doyle. "Maybe she got bored."

"You didn't have to ask for pie," said William. "Ridiculous."

"I was hungry," said Doyle. "I don't think we'll need her at this point anyway. Right now, we just need to call Amanda and the gang and hopefully get them to stop Dillhole or whatever he's calling himself before he kills another innocent person."

"Absolutely. You get in. I'll drive."

"You're just like Amanda." Doyle pulled out his cell phone.

She answered on the first ring.

"Amanda, it's Doyle. Where are you at?"

"We just finished having dinner and now we're headed towards Bismarck. Why, what's up?"

"I need you to double back towards Valley City. We have reason to believe that a Madeline Benson is a potential victim. If he hasn't gotten her already, he will soon."

"Okay," she said. He could hear Amanda speaking to someone, probably Steven. "All right, we're headed that way. What do you know about this guy?"

"You're going to love this. He's going by the name 'Eddie Dillberg.'"

"So he's a *funny* sadistic serial killer. That's great."

"You may want to hurry. I'm not sure what kind of schedule Mr. Dillberg is on. He's been accelerating, so we may already be too late."

"We'll get there as fast as we can," said Amanda. "I'll call you when we're there."

"Good," said Doyle. "Be careful."

23

The Friendly Companion was excited. The incredibly hot reporter—assuming that's what she was—had to be driving towards Bismarck. That's where he killed his third victim. Hilga Johansen was younger than he had expected and put up a heck of a fight, but he took her down in the end. He wondered what the blonde reporter thought of his work? Was she impressed? In awe? He'd ask her soon enough.

It was getting late. This was to his benefit. He'd made a big mistake by trailing the vehicle with the reporter and her crew so closely. When they pulled into the gas station and waited, he knew they'd grown suspicious. He was still behind them, but by a very safe distance. As it grew darker, he could pull up closer and can the headlights.

He adjusted the knob on the radio. That was the problem with this damn state. You drive thirty yards and lose whatever signal you'd been picking up. And too much damn country music. Every station. Was there no appreciation for classic rock nowadays?

The distraction of the radio almost got the best of him. When he glanced up he didn't see the Honda. He did a double take in the side view mirror and saw the car disappearing behind him. *Shit!* He hadn't been paying close enough attention. At some point in the last couple minutes, they must have flipped a U-turn. Where the hell were they going?

He pulled into a turn lane and made a U-turn himself. If he had to guess where they were going, they must have heard about Maddie

Benson, his most recent victim. The one that couldn't have been more obvious as the work of the Friendly Companion. The Dillman label he'd tossed on her corpse should have been a pretty good tip-off to the police. If they couldn't connect the dots from that little number, then he'd lose all faith in humanity. Okay, so he'd lost that quite some time ago.

It was getting dark enough. He turned off his headlights.

He couldn't wait to see her

24

Steven drove fast as Amanda read aloud the address Doyle had texted her.

Hanratty searched the map for the approximate neighborhood. "I think I found it."

"Let's hope so," said Amanda. "The way Doyle was talking, it sounded like the homeowner could be dead already."

"I really hope not," said Hanratty. "I hate taking pictures of dead people."

"You did that for years," said Amanda.

"Yeah, and look where it's gotten me. I'm an unemployed alcoholic with God-awful images seared into my brain. Do you know what it's like to have one of those images pop into your brain when you're trying to masturb—"

"HANRATTY!" yelled Amanda.

"Sorry. You know what I mean, though."

"How far out are we?" asked Amanda.

Steven looked at the clock. "I saw a sign for Valley City a while back. We're still forty miles away. The speed I'm driving, though, we'll be there in like ten minutes."

"Maybe you should slow down some," said Amanda. "I'd like to be alive upon arrival."

"We'll be fine," said Steven. He added even more pressure to the accelerator.

"I think I'll drive from now on," said Amanda.

Steven laughed. "Whatever you wish, partner."

* * *

"Is this the neighborhood?" asked Amanda.

"I think so," said Hanratty. "According to the map, this should be it."

"I don't see that house number on any of these houses," said Steven.

"Maybe it's in a more secluded area," said Hanratty. "Why don't you drive towards that dead end. Could be down there."

"All right," said Steven. He followed the road past several homes, each of which were separated by several lots of empty land. The house numbers were right on target.

"There it is," said Amanda. "That should be Maddie Benson's house." She looked down the street. Most of the outside lights on the houses they'd past were on, but Maddie Benson's were turned off. It didn't necessarily mean anything, but . . .

"Let's go in as a group," said Amanda. "We're not sure what we might find or if we'll be in any danger. Let's stick together."

"A little scared?" asked Steven.

"Yes," said Amanda. "Yes, I am."

"We'll be fine," said Hanratty, grabbing his camera bag. "Even if it's ugly in there, it's nothing we haven't seen before, right?"

"I just hope we made it in time," said Amanda. "I hope she's alive."

"Let's find out," said Steven.

Together, they marched up the front steps. Amanda knocked on the door, holding in her breath, praying that a sweet, little old lady might answer the door. The eerily silence that followed seemed to last forever.

25

The Friendly Companion stopped his car at the entrance of the dead end. He knew there were a couple different approaches he could take at this point. One, he could follow them to dead woman's house and add a few more corpses to the body pile. Two, he could wait for them here. After all, there was only one way out.

He was thinking perhaps the latter would be more appropriate. It might be kind of fun, too.

His crotch itched horribly. By now the effects of the pickle juice had long since dissipated, but the fresh sores that resulted from his scratching continued to itch.

However, something was also itching in the back of his brain. He was missing something. Something important.

Then it dawned on him. If she was a reporter responding to something she picked up on a police scanner or even something leaked from a contact at the police department, then, well . . . where were the police?

Unless she wasn't a reporter. Could she be a detective? If so, he could be in a very uncomfortable position. Especially if she called for back-up and he had a bunch of squads coming up behind him.

Wait—how did she find out about Maddie Benson? Unless . . . did she know? Did she really figure it out? Did she know all about the Friendly Companion and the information he got from his young, stupid girlfriend at the Garrison Bank?

If so, then he was both mystified by her intelligence and anxious about what was about to come. This was moving into the end-game much faster than he had anticipated. After months of hoping someone would put the pieces together—here it was. It'd finally happened. There wasn't much left to do now.

His instinct was to go to the house right now and put an end to them. But in the end—wasn't this what he wanted all along? For the news to get around? Maybe he'd just help them out a bit.

He reached into the workbag at his side. He pushed aside the insurance papers that were now dry but stiff and pungent from when he'd broken the jar in Maddie's home. Ahh, memories. He found what he wanted. A nightstick. It wasn't quite the same as his leather-clad fists, but it did pack a little more oomph.

The Friendly Companion sat back and waited.

26

Amanda, Steven, and Hanratty exited the house with pale, sullen faces. Hanratty had a digital file full of images he'd prefer to never see again. For Amanda and Steven, the memories were bad enough.

"Monstrous," said Steven. "Why the pickle in the mouth? That was just unnecessary."

"I need a drink," said Hanratty. "A lot of drinks."

They climbed into the car. Steven was behind the wheel, Amanda on the passenger side, and Hanratty in the backseat.

"You should call Doyle," said Steven. "Let him know what we saw. Then call the police. It's too late for Maddie, but at least the police can do their investigation."

"I feel like we're over our heads on this one," said Amanda. "Maybe we were wrong to try to take this on ourselves. Something like this—you need a whole police department working on it. Or the F.B.I. We're just a bunch of yahoos trying to do it ourselves."

"It doesn't matter now," said Steven. "We're doing the best we can. And if we're lucky, maybe we can catch this guy before he does . . . *that* . . . to someone else."

"Okay," said Amanda. "Yeah, I guess you're right. I'll call Doyle." Amanda pulled out her cell phone and dialed Doyle's number. She heard three rings followed by his voice saying, "Hello?"

As Amanda tried to respond, her world exploded. Something struck the other side of the car. Steven's side. Everything was loud and painful.

And moving. She lost all sense of what direction she was facing. Shattered glass sprayed her face.

Then, as fast as it happened, everything was still. It was dark out. She couldn't see anything. Or was something in her eyes? Blood maybe. She heard the engine hiss. And footsteps. Crunching on glass.

Doyle's voice. "Amanda? Are you okay? What's going on?"

* * *

He'd done a bang up job. The driver was limp and lifeless behind the steering wheel that dug deeply into his ribcage.

The thin man in the back was alive and trying to push open the door, but he could see the man's legs were caught under the front seat. Maybe they were crushed. He considered taking out the nightstick and giving him a few good whacks to the forehead, but then he connected eyes with the man. Fear blanketed the thin man's face. But the man still had the gall to reach for his camera.

At first, the Friendly Companion felt rage boiling within him. Then it subsided. This was it. The end-game. There was no going back now. The thin man lifted the camera and aimed it at the Friendly Companion. He smiled. And for good measure, he winked at the camera, too. But he also felt a horrible itch down yonder and instinctively scratched it just as the camera flashed. *Damn*, he thought. *That would not make for a very attractive front page shot.*

The Friendly Companion walked around to the front passenger side of the vehicle. There she was. The beauty queen. She was very much alive, although bloodied up pretty bad.

The Friendly Companion ripped open the door, released the latch on her seat belt, then yanked her to the ground. She tried to flail, but it was useless.

"No," he heard the man in the backseat say.

"Save it," he said. "She's coming with me."

"No," the thin man said again. But he wasn't going anywhere, not with those legs.

"Tell everyone you know that the Friendly Companion took your friend. Got it?"

The thin man didn't respond, but the Friendly Companion knew he'd gotten his message across.

He wrapped duct tape over the woman's mouth and around her wrists. Then he dragged her, kicking—but just barely—and popped open the trunk of his car. His front end was also smashed in, but hopefully it would still work. And if it didn't—he'd hotwired enough cars in his youth, he'd have no trouble finding another getaway car.

He threw her in the trunk, inaudible sounds buried beneath the duct tape on her mouth. He slammed the trunk shut.

Jamming the car in reverse, he hoped for the best. He knew he'd be okay. One proverb that'd followed him through his life had rarely failed him. Good things happen to bad people.

Good fortune was on his side. The car reversed.

He turned around and headed for the highway.

27

Doyle sat stunned inside William's car. They were parked outside a small rest stop in west central North Dakota. William was just coming back from the restroom.

"Oh, God," muttered Doyle. "Oh, my God."

"What's going on?" asked William, opening the driver's side door and sitting down.

"I think Amanda's been kidnapped. Or she's already dead."

"Come again?"

"I just heard horrible things. A crash. Screaming."

"Maybe she had the radio turned up too loud," said William. "On one of those heavy metal stations. That music is dreadful."

"I don't think so, William. They don't have those kinds of stations out this way. And it wasn't music I heard. I'm sure of it. I distinctly heard someone say, 'She's coming with me.'"

"Let's get going," said William.

"Didn't you hear me?" yelled Doyle.

William shrank away.

"Amanda—*my* Amanda—has been kidnapped by a deranged serial killer. We have to call the police."

"Let's not get ahead of ourselves," said William. He turned the ignition, reversed, then stomped his foot on the accelerator.

"We have to call the police," repeated Doyle. "This is my fault, William. I put her in harm's way. We have to save her from that madman."

"We will," said William. "Let's just think this through. Do we know who we're dealing with yet?"

"No," said Doyle. "Just that he's batshit insane."

"Do we know where he's headed?"

"No," said Doyle. "That house they went to . . . Maddie Benson's house? That was the last name on the list."

"So do we have any clue what's going to happen next?"

Doyle grew frustrated. "No," he said.

"Would the police know any better than us?"

Doyle lowered his head. "No."

"Exactly," said William. "Let's get our rear ends there as soon as possible. We'll find out what happened and then formulate a plan. Don't worry, Doyle. We'll get her back."

"We better," said Doyle.

"We will," said William.

* * *

Twenty minutes later, Doyle was so lost in his own thoughts—mostly regarding all the horrible things that were most certainly happening or would soon be happening to Amanda—that he jumped out of his skin when his cell phone rang. It was from Amanda's phone.

"Amanda? Is that you? Are you okay?"

"Doyle—it's Hanratty. He's taken Amanda. She's gone, Doyle."

Numerous expletives raced through Doyle's mind, but nothing came out of his mouth.

"Are you still there, Doyle?"

"Yeah. I'm still here. What happened?"

"He was waiting for us outside the Benson home. Rammed our car with his. Steven's in pretty rough shape, but he should live. My legs might be broken. They hurt bad."

"Hanratty, what did he do with Amanda?"

"He gagged her and threw her in his trunk."

"Do you have the make and model of the vehicle? A license plate?"

"No, Doyle, I'm sorry. I was pinned in. I still am. I really couldn't get a good view. The ambulance should be here any minute."

"Okay, good," said Doyle. "I'm glad help's on the way."

"I have one thing that might help you, though," said Hanratty. "Actually, it'll probably help you a lot."

"What's that?"

"I have his photograph."

"You do? How did you get that?" asked Doyle.

"He let me take it," said Hanratty.

"That's incredible," said Doyle. "Okay, we'll meet you at the hospital. Just don't let anyone take your camera or the memory card or Polaroid or whatever the heck you used."

"You got it, Doyle."

"Did you recognize him?"

"No," said Hanratty. "But he seemed to have some sort of skin disease. Or maybe an STD. He was scratching his crotch. A lot."

"That's odd," said Doyle. Then he thought of Amanda and what this maniac might do to her. "Holy crap. We have to help Amanda right away!"

"She's a strong woman, Doyle. She'll be okay. Just get here as fast as you can."

"You got it, buddy. I'll see you soon, Hanratty. I hope your legs are going to be okay."

"It's cool," said Hanratty. "Since I lost my job as a bike cop, I haven't been using them too much."

Doyle hung up.

"What's going on?" asked William. He was clocking over ninety miles per hour, well on the way to one hundred.

"Hanratty has a photo of the killer. The guy let him take it."

William groaned.

"What? What is it?"

"That's a terrible sign," said William. "It means he doesn't care if he gets caught. He could do anything at this point. There are no boundaries."

William must have seen the look on Doyle's face, because he backtracked.

"But of course Amanda will be just fine," said William. "I think the chances of this Friendly Companion fellow hurting Amanda are . . . minimal."

"Thanks, William. That really puts me at ease."

"No problem, Doyle. Happy to help. Perhaps I'll speed up a wee bit."

"You're going to go faster? Oh, boy. Apparently you feel this is a little more urgent than you're letting on?"

"Not in the least. I'm simply testing the tread on my wheels. They're still under warranty, and I want to ensure they're as good as advertised."

"It has nothing to do with the fact that my girlfriend has been kidnapped by a madman who may or may not have a venereal disease?"

"Not at all," said William. "Wait—venereal disease?"

"He keeps scratching his crotch, apparently."

"Huh," said William. "That's an interesting detail. Not sure what it means, but good to know nonetheless."

"Hopefully it means nothing to Amanda, if you know what I mean."

"I doubt it. Our copycat fellow punches, shoots, and kills people. He doesn't rape them."

"You're so, so comforting William. Thanks," said Doyle, shaking his head.

"Glad to be of service. Stop worrying. We'll have her back, none the worse for wear."

28

Amanda gained consciousness with a mighty jolt when her tiny, dark prison seemed to drop about two feet. She'd never been too politically involved before, but she was definitely about to take up lobbying for sufficient pothole repair funding. If she ever got out of this. Christ, her head was splitting.

She was disappointed in herself for having lost consciousness. Without knowing how long she had been out, she had no way of estimating how far they'd traveled. If she ever had any chance of contacting the world outside of this musky trunk, she'd be of little help saying where she was.

Her cell phone. Did she still have it? Her hands were bound behind her, but she could feel her phone wasn't in her back pocket. It'd probably fallen out when she was yanked out of her car.

Wait—wasn't she talking to Doyle at the time? Yes. Did Doyle hear everything? Would he be able to figure out what had happened? He wasn't the sharpest tool in the shed, but he got lucky sometimes. Hopefully he'd have some luck on his side this time.

The driver took a sharp turn, and something hit Amanda in the face. Several somethings, in fact. Small tubes. Squishy. Toothpaste, maybe? No, it smelled much stronger than that. Almost metallic. Was it ointment? Oh, God—what did that mean?

Suddenly, the car stopped. A door opened then closed. Footsteps came closer. Then, the trunk opened, letting a brilliant wave of sunlight.

She tried to see the killer. It was too bright. She heard him, though. Scratching. What was he scratching?

The only thing she saw was his hand reach down and grab one of the tubes by her face. "Patience," he whispered to her. Followed by, "Damn junk." What did that mean? Was she just junk to him? Typical serial killer thought patterns, she thought. The trunk slammed shut.

Then she heard footsteps fading into background. Then a loud knocking. Then his voice again. Yelling. But not at her. Someone else. She could make it out, but just barely. "Honey, I'm home!"

Thirty seconds later, she heard two gunshots. Footsteps coming back. Then the ignition.

They were moving again. Amanda prayed for her safety, and for very few potholes.

29

oyle and William reached the Jamestown Regional Medical Center just before midnight. The hospital was fairly large for the size of the town it was located in. Doyle assumed it must serve a much larger population than just Jamestown. People were likely brought in from several cities away for anything small local clinics couldn't handle.

At the front desk, a scrub-clad middle-aged woman with her hair pulled back into a bun greeted them with a tiny rigid smile and suspicious eyes.

"Good evening, gentlemen. How can I help you?"

"Hi, ma'am. We're here to see Glenn Hanratty and Steven Kanter."

"The men from the car wreck?"

"Yes, that's them," said William.

"Are you family?" asked the woman, glancing back and forth between Doyle and William.

"Not exactly," said Doyle.

"Then I can't let you in," said the woman. "I'm sorry."

"I don't think you understand," said Doyle. "We're not family, per se, but Steven and I . . . well, we're—" Doyle leaned in close to her and whispered, "partners."

"Partners?" she whispered back. "You mean . . . cops?"

"Well, yes," said Doyle.

"Still not good enough. You got to be family to get in."

"Ma'am, we're not just that kind of partners, if you know what I mean."

The woman furrowed her brow and shook her head.

"Doyle's gay, ma'am," said William. "So is Steven. You're not going to discriminate, are you?"

The woman blushed and shook her head, more vehemently this time. "No, no of course not."

They began to walk down the hall.

"Wait! What about you?" She was looking at William.

He sighed. "I'm gay, too. The other fellow who was in the crash is my partner."

"The thin guy who keeps begging for Leinenkugel's?"

"Yes, him. I have low standards. Okay?"

She nodded. "Okay. Down the hall. Take a right, then it's the last door on the left."

"Thanks," said William. "C'mon Doyle. I'm sure Steven's been missing you."

"Same with your Glenny Wenny, right William?"

"Keep walking."

Despite the playful banter, Doyle wasn't thrilled about being in a hospital again. His worst experience in a hospital, as well as one of his most painful memories, was shortly after his dad had been shot by a street thug in Minneapolis. Doyle had a chance to see him for a brief period in the Hennepin County Medical Center. Harry Malloy wasn't conscious at that point, which may have been for the better. Doyle was never good in emotional situations.

Last year, Doyle saw William almost murdered in a hospital. They thought it was William's ex-wife, Eva, who tried to take his life, but it turned out to be a madman. To be fair, it was really hard to tell the difference.

"We were in a hospital just like this last year, remember?"

"Don't remind me," said William.

"Too late. Hopefully Steven or Hanratty won't try to kill you."

"I think I'll be okay. I feel more sorry that they'd almost been killed."

"I hear you."

William looked at Doyle curiously. "Have you been having audial problems?"

Doyle shook his head. "It's an American expression. Never mind. Hey, I think that's the room."

Hanratty's voice floated into the hall. He was yelling. "I don't care if it's out of season. I'm in the hospital. I need a case of Summer Shandy's. STAT."

William knocked on the door.

Doyle stuck his head in. "What's going on, Hanratty?"

Hanratty was lying in his hospital bed, his legs raised in a sling. He had casts and white tape all over his body. He brought a finger to his lips. "Shhh. I'm on the phone with a local liquor store. I'm placing an order." He turned his attention away from Doyle and William. "Fine. Make it Oktoberfest. Just bring it to the hospital. Hurry it up. I'm dyin' here. I might not have much time left." He hung up.

"Can you believe they barely carry any Leinie's in this state?" asked Hanratty.

Doyle had visited the Leinenkugel's brewery in Chippewa Falls, Wisconsin, many times in his twenties. Despite the fact that it was now owned by a major conglomerate, it could still be difficult to find their brews in some areas. Especially when you really, really needed one.

"I understand, Hanratty," said Doyle. "And I won't even complain this time. You deserve a Leinie's."

"God, it's good to hear that," said Hanratty.

"Where's Steven?" asked William.

"Oh," said Hanratty. "He's behind the curtain."

"Is he okay?" asked Doyle.

"Maybe," said Hanratty. "He hasn't gained consciousness yet. It's too early to tell."

Doyle walked into the room and William followed. Doyle pulled back the white curtain, exposing a badly damaged Steven Kanter. The heavy bandages wrapped around his head were the most troubling to Doyle.

"He'll be okay," said Hanratty. "He's a fighter. I'm not too worried."

Doyle imagined what kind of condition Amanda must be in by now. Was she as badly damaged as Steven? Doyle wasn't as concerned about the physical damage as much as the emotional. He couldn't stand to think of her becoming any less sunny, optimistic, or humorous than she usually was. These thoughts swirled through Doyle's head before finally settling and helping him focus on his mission.

"Hanratty—you said you have a photo of the killer? The guy who kidnapped Amanda?"

"I do," said Hanratty. "I couldn't believe he let me take it. I assumed he was just going to kill me and be done with it. Just goes to show ya."

William crumpled his eyebrows. "It goes to show you what?"

Hanratty shrugged. "Crazy people are unpredictable. Now, I have to warn you. Shortly after I called you, the ambulance showed up, along with the local police. The police in this town did a surprisingly thorough job. Apparently they located Maddie Benson's body not too long after they arrived at the crash site. I'm not sure how they found out about Ms. Benson. Maybe they figured out that's where our car had been, or maybe the killer called it in himself. Who knows. Either way, they were very suspicious of both me and Steven. So they confiscated everything, including my camera."

Doyle groaned. William let loose a torrent of British-accented expletives.

"But it's okay guys. The one thing they didn't take was my cell phone. I transferred the file to my phone as I sat in the backseat of the car, my legs feeling like Gallagher's watermelons."

William shot a curious glance at Doyle, but he waved him away. Obviously, William didn't pick up on the reference.

"That's amazing, Hanratty," said Doyle. "It's unbelievable you were able to do that."

"Thanks. I'm pretty great sometimes."

"Well," said Doyle. "Let's see it."

Hanratty slowly moved his arm and grimaced in pain. "Top drawer," he said, pointing at the small bureau next to the bed.

William walked over and opened the drawer, then pulled out the small, black cell phone. He flipped it open.

"Hit the little picture button on the bottom right," said Hanratty.

William did. "Oh, my," he said.

"What is it?" asked Doyle.

"Oh, my," William repeated. He handed the phone to Doyle.

Doyle looked down at the small photograph on the phone's screen. "It's kinda fuzzy," said Doyle. "But he certainly doesn't look too nice. That's quite the grimace."

"Doyle, please tell me you recognize him," said William.

Doyle stared hard at the photograph. "Err . . . I don't think I do. Why, do you?"

"Absolutely."

"You do? Who is it? Have we met him?"

"Not exactly."

"Then who the hell is it?"

"Before we left for North Dakota, what was one of the last things we did?"

"I picked up Hanratty at the Martiniapolis Tavern," said Doyle.

"Okay, you did that. What about before that?"

"I had a lovely visit with Amanda's boss."

"Okay, before that?"

"I had amazing sex with Amanda. She did that thing I like where she—"

"Before that?"

"That previous night we were at Clara Belmont's house," said Doyle.

"Did you get a good look at her house?" asked William.

"Yeah. It was really neat and tidy. Too much so. Creepy."

"Did you see any photographs in her house?"

"Well . . . I guess I didn't really look that closely."

"Oh, Doyle. Someday you'll learn."

"Save that for later. Are you saying this is Clara Belmont's husband?"

"That's exactly what I'm saying," said William.

"Unbelievable," said Doyle. "So Unlucky Larry's son-in-law is the copycat killer. And we've established that this copycat has used a gun on at least a couple of the victims. Maybe he shot Unlucky Larry too?"

"Let's not jump to too many conclusions," said William.

"So the cases are connected," said Doyle. "I was right! How about that? Wait until I tell Amanda!"

William glared at Doyle.

"We should go find her now," said Doyle. "Where do we go? Should we try Clara Belmont's house?"

"Seems like as good a place as any."

"Should we call the police first?" asked Doyle. "They could be there a lot faster than we can."

"You're right, but I don't think it'll make any difference. I can get us there in a couple hours. We should go."

"William, I know getting credit for the work we do is important to you, but I think the police might be really necessary this time."

William sighed. "I'll leave it up to you, Doyle. It's Amanda's life on the line, after all. Whatever you think is best."

"Okay," said Doyle. "Let me go use the bathroom first."

An unexpectedly loud intercom chirped. The unpleasant voice of the woman at the front desk said, "Mr. Hanratty—we have a special delivery for you. Since it's not allowed on the premises, I'll keep it stored in the employee's room until you're ready to leave the hospital."

Hanratty looked at William. "While Doyle goes to the bathroom, you go get my beer. Use your gun if you have to."

"I'll take care of it," said William.

"I'll be right back," said Doyle. First, he approached Hanratty and wrapped his arms around him. Hanratty flinched, then relaxed. "Thanks for everything, including not dying."

"Don't mention it," said Hanratty, grinding his teeth. "Less hugging, though. It's not that I don't appreciate it. I'm just in a world of pain."

"Oh, sorry. Take care, buddy. I'll see you soon."

"Go get the bastard, Doyle."

Doyle nodded. As Doyle left the room, he saw William shake hands with Hanratty. Doyle went into the hall and found a sign for the restrooms. He slipped inside and turned the water faucets on full blast to cover up any noise. He pulled out his cell phone and dialed 411.

"I need the number for the police department in Golden Valley, Minnesota. Please transfer me. It's urgent."

Moments later, he was connected with a dispatcher.

"Hi, there. I think I saw somebody break into the house of my neighbor, Clara Belmont. That's Belmont. Right. Please have someone go check on her. House number? I don't . . . gotta go."

Doyle hung up. He put the phone back in his pocket, then turned off the faucets. He walked into the hallway. William was walking toward him with a case of beer in one hand and a gun in the other. The woman from the front desk, now seething angry, watched with her arms folded.

"All set to go?" asked William, heading back into Hanratty and Steven's room.

Doyle realized he did actually have to pee. It was going to be a long drive. Doyle retreated back into the bathroom and took care of business

30

The drive to Golden Valley was one of the longest Doyle ever had to endure. Physically it was no longer than any of the other routes they'd taken during the course of the weekend, but Doyle felt exhausted from so much driving—or rather, riding in his case—and he felt the anxiety over Amanda was mounting and taking its toll on him.

"I have to warn you, Doyle, that things may not be as peachy as you'd like them to be. I know you want to swoop in and save Amanda. But whatever it is we find in the Belmont house—just be aware that it may not be good. You have to be mentally prepared for that."

"You certainly know how to say the right things, William. I've never felt so relaxed."

"Really?"

"Good God, no. I'm ready to jump out of my skin. I have no doubt the images playing in my head are probably far worse than what we're actually going to find. I'm hoping and praying Amanda will be fine. But whatever the case, I assure you my mind's playing out every scenario in my head. I can't wait to know the truth and let all these crazy thoughts just go away."

"Very well," said William. "As long as you're prepared. That's all I'm asking. I'd hate to see you fall apart."

"You're really terrible at this," said Doyle. "You think there's any chance in hell I wouldn't 'fall apart' if the . . . you know, worst case scenario turned out to be the truth?"

"I suppose not," said William.

"Sorry," said Doyle. "I'm a little on edge. In case you couldn't tell."

"It's okay. I would be, too. I am myself. Amanda's wonderful. I don't want to see anything bad befall her."

"Same here," said Doyle. "Can you drive any faster?"

* * *

When they reached the Belmont neighborhood in Golden Valley, Doyle's heart sank. He was expecting to see at least a squad car or two because of the call he made. He was not expecting to see an ambulance, several squads, two fire trucks, and even a few media vans with ridiculously tall antennas.

"Brace yourself, Doyle," said William. "Obviously something happened here, but it may not have anything to do with Amanda."

Doyle felt nauseous when he saw a stretcher being rolled out the front door. A body was on the stretcher, covered in a white sheet. The EMTs were not attempting any sort of resuscitation. Whoever was on that stretcher had croaked.

Outside the ambulance, Doyle saw a familiar face. She was taking notes.

"William, park the car. I need to go talk to someone."

"Okay, Doyle. Be careful. Don't do anything stupid."

"When have I ever . . . ? Never mind, just park."

Doyle bolted out of the car. William had parked up on a hill. Doyle ran downhill, a little faster than intended.

"Razor! Ms. Razor! Err . . . Cynthia! It's Doyle! I have to—whoops," Doyle yelped as his feet got tangled on his downward descent. Before he knew what was happening, he was rolling down the hill towards the Belmont's front yard. When he skidded to a stop, several guns were pointed directly at him.

Doyle held up his hands, reached in his coat, and pulled out his P.I. license. "I'm Detective Doyle Malloy. I just need to speak to Razor here for a minute." His use of her nickname caused a few snickers from the other cops.

Chief Cynthia Reiser signaled the other cops to lower their weapons. "Malloy, stand up. You're embarrassing yourself."

Doyle stood. He pointed at the stretcher. "Who—?"

"Have a nice trip?" asked Reiser.

Doyle immediately assumed she knew about their activities in North Dakota. Then he realized what she was referring to. "Oh, you mean the hill."

"Yes, I mean the hill. What are you doing here, Malloy? I thought I made myself perfectly clear that you and Amanda had nothing further to do with this investigation?"

Doyle again pointed at the stretcher. "Who exactly is—"

"No, I think I'll ask the questions first. Why are you here?"

Doyle wasn't sure what he should say. William wasn't beside him. He looked up the hill and saw William standing outside the vehicle. William nodded. Even though William clearly couldn't hear their conversation, Doyle took it as a signal that it was okay to talk.

"I've been tracking a serial killer," explained Doyle.

"Oh?" Reiser lifted her notepad. She suddenly seemed far more interested in what Doyle had to say.

"He's a copycat of the—hold on. Wait a minute. I have to do this," said Doyle. He walked over to the stretcher, pulled back the sheet, and stared into the lifeless eyes of Clara Belmont. She had two sizeable holes in her head that were not there the previous evening.

"Thank God," said Doyle.

"You're relieved?" asked Reiser. "What exactly is going on here?"

"Amanda was with me. And Steven. They decided to help me out during their involuntary time off," said Doyle.

Reiser pursed her lips.

"Anyway, we became aware of a copycat killer. He'd been modeling his murders after the Friendly Companion from back in the eighties. Are you familiar with him?"

"The pickle guy. Sure."

"The copycat's been responsible for six murders in North Dakota. It appears his wife is the seventh."

Reiser looked at the ambulance which now contained the seventh victim. The ambulance took off down the road.

"Are you saying Clara Belmont's husband is the copycat killer? Are you positive?"

"We have proof. We have his photograph, taken shortly after he destroyed Amanda's car and kidnapped her."

Reiser jaw dropped. "Holy shit."

"I need your help, Cynthia. I know you don't care for me. But we have to get Amanda back before Belmont does whatever he's planning."

"Do you have any idea where he's gone?" Reiser clenched her fists. Her face reddened. "You have to tell me whatever you know. You better not hold back on me."

"I have no idea. I was hoping you could tell me. We only thought he might come here."

"The only thing I know is that a neighbor saw Clara's husband's car arrive then leave a few minutes later. We're already working on tracking his car down."

"How can I help?" asked Doyle. "What can I do?"

"You need to give me everything you have. I need the photograph."

"We have a lot more than that," said Doyle. "We have photographic evidence from most of his victims. Only problem is, the Jamestown police have possession of it. You'll have to get it from them."

"Damn it," said Reiser, kicking a rock on the driveway. "That's fine. We'll deal with that later. We'll work on locating him. I'll work with the other agencies. We'll get everyone on this."

"What can I do?" repeated Doyle.

"I think you've done plenty, Malloy," said Reiser. "The best thing you can do at this point is get out of our way while we conduct a complete investigation and find Detective Hutchins. Anything else you do at this point will just be getting in the way."

Doyle didn't like what he heard, but ultimately was not surprised. He couldn't have expected much different.

"Will you keep me posted on everything you find out?" asked Doyle.

"Of course I will, Doyle. You should go get some sleep. You look exhausted."

Doyle realized he hadn't slept for more than a couple hours all weekend. Mostly in the car. "Sure. I can do that."

"Good. Take care, Detective. Don't worry—I'll find Amanda."

Reiser pursed her lips again, then went back to taking notes.

"I don't think you'll find Amanda in that notebook," said Doyle, walking uphill towards the car. "Just an FYI."

31

Amanda didn't know at what point she had conked out again. She had little air in the trunk, it was dark, and her head got smacked around every time the bastard hit a pothole, which was often. She wondered if he was intentionally aiming for them.

She didn't know what her chances were of getting out of this, but she hoped that, no matter what happened, that Doyle would be okay. She didn't want him to fall to pieces. Despite years on the police force and as private detective, he was still a fragile guy.

Amanda decided she better go ahead and survive. If not for her own sake, then for Doyle's. He could barely put his pants on without her.

The car stopped. Not good. Last time, she thought he'd shot and killed someone. Was she next? Or were they stopping so he could get out and slay someone else?

The car door opened and slammed shut. Then she heard nothing. The silence seemed to stretch on forever. Then she heard something. Metallic sounds. *Clinking. Clanking.* Then a different car roared to life.

The trunk opened. The light hurt her eyes, but she focused enough that she could see they were in a parking garage.

"Don't make a sound." The voice was cold. Unfriendly. The same man who pulled her out of her car a few hours ago. Or was it a few days? She had no clue.

He looked familiar. Why was that? Her head was too foggy. She couldn't think.

He reached for her. She flinched, but didn't scream. Then his arms were under her. Lifting.

She looked around. Lots of cars in the lot. They had North Dakota license plates. That was good. At least she could narrow down which state she was in. Most of the cars were older. Rusty. Junky. Some had stickers on their bumpers. NDSU. North Dakota State University. They must be in Fargo.

As excited as she was to be out of that God-awful trunk, she knew she was going from the frying pan to the fire. The killer dropped her in a different trunk, just to the right of the car they'd been in.

"It won't be much longer now," he said. His hand moved to his pants. At first she feared the worst—that he was going to do something altogether inappropriate and invasive right then and there. Then she realized he was scratching. And he was most certainly not enjoying himself. His face was red. He was almost in tears.

"Fucking pickles," he screamed as he slammed the trunk shut.

Back in the dark, Amanda wondered what was happening to the crazy man who'd kidnapped her. Clearly something was amiss in his khakis, and pickles appeared to be the culprit. Did he try to do something of a sexual nature to a jar of pickles? Seemed unlikely, but then again, this guy didn't really seem to be playing with a full deck. Maybe he was simply having a reaction. But to pickles? That would be awfully ironic.

The car began moving. Amanda dreaded what was to come. More darkness. More potholes. Hopefully this vehicle had better suspension.

The killer took a quick left and Amanda rolled, banging into the rear portion of the trunk. Her arm hit something sharp. She was probably bleeding. What was that?

Despite the pain, she reached back with her duct-tape bound hands. They were numb, but she wanted to get a sense of what had hurt her. It felt like a piece of really sharp plastic that came out from underneath the cheap upholstery in the trunk. Not very safe, but then again, not many people rode inside a trunk. Voluntarily, anyway.

She reached behind her again, but this time rested the duct-tape binding her wrists against the plastic. She dragged her arms back and forth, desperately hoping the plastic would be sharp enough to cut through the tape. It didn't help that she couldn't see what she was doing, or if her plan was being effective. She continued for a few minutes, then tried to pull her hands apart. To her disappointment, she didn't feel any give.

The killer hit a pothole and Amanda's head hammered against the floor. She nearly lost consciousness again. She shook her head and reached back. She pressed the tape firmly on the plastic, then pushed down with all her strength and moved her arms back and forth, back and forth, back and forth.

This time she heard the tape ripping. The sound made her excited and nervous, since she knew that if she was lucky enough to cut through the tape, she could end up with sharp plastic cutting into her wrist, and who knows how much blood she could lose as a result.

When she thought she couldn't rock against the tape one more time, she rolled to her side, then with all the strength she could muster, she pulled her arms apart.

The sound of the tape splitting was like a bag of potato chips being ripped open. Oh, it was glorious.

Amanda shifted, trying to bring the blood back into her hands. They tingled painfully. But she also felt a huge sense of freedom. And hope.

32

hat should I do now?" asked Doyle.

William was in the driver's seat. His typical five-o'clock shadow was looking more like a midnight shadow. His eyes were bloodshot.

"By the way, you look terrible," said Doyle.

"Have you seen yourself lately?"

Doyle grabbed the rear view mirror and turned it toward himself so he could see his reflection. He leaned away in horror. "Ahh!"

"You've been awake, more or less, for the last forty-eight hours. You may want to consider getting some sleep."

"C'mon, William. You know that's impossible with Amanda out there . . . somewhere. I can't just grab some beauty rest."

"Sure you can. Because I'll keep working."

"What do you mean?"

"I've been through this before. Usually it's just a matter of putting out all the pieces of the puzzle onto the table, then figuring out how they fit together. I'm not sure what our copycat is doing with Amanda, but I'm sure he has a game plan. He's been rather organized thus far. I just need to deduce what his next move is."

"I can help you," said Doyle.

"You'll be of little help in your current condition," said William. "Go home. Get a couple hours of real rest. Then we can take it from there."

"I don't know . . ."

"Just do it. Trust me. You'll feel better."

Doyle sighed. "If you come up with anything, let me know immediately. Okay?"

"Absolutely," said William.

* * *

Doyle's head hit the pillow. It still smelled like Amanda. Doyle choked back a sob, but it didn't take long before he gave into relentless exhaustion. The past couple days had taken their toll physically and mentally. He only hoped that when he awoke, he'd have a renewed focus and maybe some idea as to where he could find the love of his life.

Sleep wrapped around him like a warm blanket. He lost himself in it, falling into a dream. He saw himself with his arms wrapped around a woman. It wasn't Amanda. It was a brunette with her hair in a bun. It was Mae Sanderson, or rather, a younger version. She was bawling her eyes out. "I'm sorry, I'm sorry," she repeated. Doyle realized his arms weren't around Mae, but rather the arms of his father, Harry.

Then he was inside a squad car patrolling downtown Garrison, on Main Street. Then something must have happened, because the car he was in squealed down a side road and came to a stop in front of a small, but well-kept house. Three other squads pulled in at the same time.

The front door was open. An old woman stood inside with a rolling pin in her hand. A body lay on the floor with wrists and feet bound. The woman also held a jar of pickles.

Doyle saw his father lift the man on the floor to his feet. Anger and hatred burned in the man's eyes. He also caught the faint scent of vinegar and dill. This was him—the original Friendly Companion. Fred Dillman.

Doyle's father dragged the murderer back to the squad car and not-so-gently threw him into the backseat. Harry Malloy got into the driver's seat and adjusted the rear view mirror so he could keep an eye on Dillman.

Before he put the squad in reverse, he glanced towards the woman in the doorway. She looked scared. Terrified. As Harry Malloy drove away, although it would be physically impossible for him to hear such a thing, Doyle heard the unmistakable sound of the lock on the doorknob being turned, followed by the heavy sliding of the deadbolt. The old woman was making her home a fortress.

He heard the locks being set over and over and over again until his eyes snapped open.

His phone was ringing. He reached for the sound and picked up the phone. He didn't recognize the number.

"Hel—" Doyle coughed. "Hello?"

"Detective Malloy? This is Chief Reiser."

"Razor—what's happening? Did you find her?"

"I'm afraid not," she said. "We did, however, find the car that belonged to Richard Belmont. It was found in an underground parking garage in the main campus of NDSU."

"I doubt he's a college student," said Doyle. "Why would he leave the car there?"

"I assume that he switched vehicles," said Reiser. "No one has reported a car stolen yet, but it's only a matter of time. By the time afternoon classes get out, we may know for sure what vehicle he's driving."

"It may be too late by then," said Doyle.

"Do you have any other suggestions?" asked Reiser.

Doyle thought about it. Specifically, he thought about his dream.

"Maybe. I need to talk to my partner first, though. I'll call you back."

"If you know something, you better tell me immediately."

"It's just a hunch. I'll call you," said Doyle, disconnecting the line.

Holding the phone, he scrolled down through the names until he landed on the one marked "William." He dialed. After two rings, he heard a hoarse response. "What? Hello? I'm here."

"William?" asked Doyle. "Were you sleeping?"

William snorted. "Absolutely not. I was working. I daresay, I may have rested my eyes for a few moments, but really, I have been working tirelessly."

"Apparently not that tirelessly," said Doyle.

He heard a sigh on the other end.

"What is it, Doyle? Have you found out anything from the police chief? Did you get some rest?"

"Yes to both," said Doyle. "We know that our copycat, Richard Belmont, switched cars at a college in Fargo. I guess he stuck Amanda into the new vehicle, too. They don't have a make or model of the car yet, though."

"Okay, well, at least it's something," said William.

"But . . . I think I may have better than that," said Doyle.

"Oh?"

"I've been doing a lot of thinking. And sleeping, which may have been even more important. Anyway, I've been thinking about Belmont and what he's been doing. He's been copying what Fred Dillman did years ago."

"Right, except now Belmont has run out of names he'd received from his bank teller girlfriend," said William.

"True," said Doyle. "But, what if he intends to 'one-up' Dillman? Become an even better Friendly Companion? What would he do?"

"Succeed where Dillman failed," said William.

"Exactly," said Doyle. "Which means he'd do what?"

"Kill the old lady who clunked Dillman over the head and handed him to the police," said William.

"What do you think?"

A few moments of silence passed. "It's possible," said William. "I'll be honest. It's better than anything I've come up with so far. But how does Amanda play into this plan of his?"

"I don't know," said Doyle. "Maybe he doesn't, either. Maybe Amanda was an afterthought. A spontaneous kidnapping."

"Perhaps. If anything, it certainly can't hurt to contact the old woman and have her be on high alert. What was her name again?"

"Something Myrtle," said Doyle. "Edna Myrtle. I remember talking with Mae Sanderson about her when we interviewed her in Garrison. She said she didn't know if Edna was still alive or not, but she definitely didn't have an account with the bank anymore."

"I'll make some calls and see what I can find," said William. "Why don't you get here as soon as possible."

"Are we going on another thrilling adventure to North Dakota?" asked Doyle.

"I'm afraid so," said William.

"Okay, I'll be right over. Just don't fall asleep in the meantime."

"I wasn't sleeping, for Heaven's sake. I was . . . what do the kids call it nowadays? Chillaxing. Yes, I was chillaxing."

"See you soon, William."

33

Amanda knew something was happening. Despite her tight, dark quarters, she found she was surprisingly aware of what was going on around her. Probably not too different than when someone who goes blind claims that their other senses have been magnified as a result. She couldn't see what the landscape looked like, but she could tell that they hadn't taken any exits—it'd been a straight shot. Based on the spastic, rapid movements of the vehicle, she guessed that her deranged kidnapper was likely running out of gas. Her dad showed her the same technique when she was growing up. When the vehicle is low on gas, whip the vehicle quickly from side to side. That'll ensure that any lingering droplets or fumes of gas in the tank get used, keeping the vehicle running the extra mile.

If he pulled into a gas station, he might open the trunk. If he did, she'd have to be ready. It might be her only chance to pull something off.

The car shifted wildly to the right. Was he exiting the freeway?

Amanda rubbed her hands, wrists, and ankles, as well as the area surrounding her mouth. The duct tape she'd been able get off had also ripped the top layer of her skin in the process. She was raw and sore, but ready to kick some ass.

The car was turned, slowed, then came to a stop. Did he make it to a station? Or was he totally out of gas? What would he do if they were stranded on the road? Would he just leave her there to rot?

Then she heard clanking noises followed by the whooshing of liquid flowing into the tank. They'd made it to a gas station. Would he open the trunk? She had no idea if he was the only customer, or if they were at a truck stop surrounded by dozens of truck drivers.

When the gasoline came to a dripping halt, she heard more clanking followed by the car door opening and shutting. Then the ignition. They were leaving.

Her heart sank. She thought maybe she had an opportunity. Now it was gone.

Then he surprised her. Instead of following the same path, he took another right. Where was he going? Behind the gas station?

The car slowed and stopped. The car door opened. Footsteps.

This might be it. Now or never.

The jingle of keys. A clink. Light poured in as the trunk lifted.

Amanda clenched her fist and threw it forward with all her strength. It came in contact with something very soft and gelatinous. He screamed. Amanda was shocked to see his face appear right next to hers. The killer was holding his crotch. When she punched him, he must have doubled over involuntarily. So she did the most logical thing she could think of. She brought her fist upwards in a quick vertical motion. It made direct contact with his jaw, making an ugly cracking sound. He dropped to the ground, squirming and squealing.

Amanda leapt out of trunk. He tried to grab for her ankles, but she was too quick. She ran around the building. The station was tiny. No other vehicles anywhere. Just a bicycle leaning next to the building.

She realized she should've jumped in the driver's seat of the car she'd been trapped in for who knows how many hours. Her instinct had been to get as far away from the killer as possible. It made her sick that her instincts may have failed her.

Charging in the front entrance, she yelled at the young man behind the counter. Not as panicked damsel in distress, but in her serious do-as-your-told cop voice. "Call the police right now," she said. "A murderer is outside your building."

The young man—more of a kid, really—looked like a deer in headlights.

"Do it now," she repeated.

He picked up the phone. In a less stressful situation, she might have snickered at the fact he was rotary dialing. She hadn't seen one of those in years.

"Do you have a gun?" she asked.

The young man shook his head.

"'At's too vad," said an ugly, distorted voice from behind her. He stood in the doorway. The mess of brown hair on his head went in every direction. His suit was disheveled. A blood-stained dress shirt was half tucked in. A tie hung loosely around his neck like a noose before an execution. His jaw had swelled and darkened. His legs were shaking. Was he still in that much pain? God, she hoped so.

To her dismay, she saw he was holding a handgun.

Despite her years of training, she started to panic. She reached out and grabbed anything she could get her hands on. A jar of spaghetti sauce. She whipped it at him. It hit the floor two feet in front of him.

He laughed. "'Eally?"

A jar of grape jelly sailed too wide and hit the cash register. A plastic bottle of mayonnaise hit the killer's shoe then bounced right off.

"'At almos hurt," he said.

A glass jar of Aunt Jemima syrup made contact with the glass door, shattering it.

The killer scowled. He held up the gun and pointed it at her.

She grabbed another jar, and before she threw it, she realized what she had. Images of the ointment in the trunk of the first car, as well as the constant scratching the killer was doing. It was because of this. Pickles. A giant jar of pickles.

Amanda looked at the young man behind the counter. "Get down!"

The killer whipped his attention over to the clerk. It was just enough time for Amanda to let loose the jar of pickles. Her aim was dead on. It made a nasty thud as it hit the killer's forehead. The jar didn't shatter, but it cracked, releasing juice all down the killer's face and chest, soaking his shirt.

The impact was substantial enough that he might have passed out but for the reaction he was having. The killer's hands flew up to his face, scratching and tearing at his own skin. The gun clattered to the floor.

Amanda sprinted towards it. She scooped it up and was about to dodge straight out the door when the killer grabbed her by the neck and slammed her to the ground.

He was on her, whimpering as they wrestled for the gun.

Amanda was losing the fight. She was strong, but he was stronger. She let the gun go, and instead grabbed the cracked jar of pickles.

He aimed the gun at her, but she knocked his hand to the side with the jar of pickles before he could get a shot off. He growled, but didn't drop the gun.

Amanda launched herself out the door. Her only chance was to get to the car before he did. A shot rang out behind her. She was closing in on the car. She heard another shot, followed by a sharp, piercing pain in her right ankle. She dropped and skidded across the ground.

Amanda clawed her way to the car. She was only a couple yards away from the rear tire when he grabbed her hair and pulled her up to her knees.

"You 'eally fucked up 'is time."

Then something hard made contact with the back of her skull and she lost her ability to fight back as darkness claimed her.

34

oyle arrived at the batcave in his classic Ford Taurus. He was still tired, but felt the adrenaline and excitement of nearing the end of his case. Of course, this one had all the more riding on it since Amanda's life was on the line.

When Doyle opened the front door to the office, he heard yelling. William was on the phone.

"How can she not have a phone? Well, send someone over then. Who? I don't care. Whoever you have patrolling the streets. You don't have anyone? Go over there yourself then! Just let her know a serial killer might be on the way and she should be aware of it. I really don't care if you're having a committee meeting for the upcoming Dickens festival. This is far more important. I told you—I'm a detective!"

William hung up. "Bloody hell."

"So I take it you didn't get hold of Edna Myrtle?"

"No, I'm afraid not," said William. "I've confirmed that she's alive and kicking, but she might not be for long depending on whether or not someone out there heeds my advice. Why are they so interested in Dickens and not a vicious serial killer?"

"You got me, William. What should we do?"

"Let's get in the car."

"Are we going? To North Dakota?"

"Have any better ideas?" asked William.

"No, not really. I can't say I'm looking forward to doing that trip again, but if we can save Amanda . . ."

"You're quite the white knight, Doyle. Riding in a car through non-treacherous territory to save your girlfriend."

Doyle shrugged. "At least Hanratty understands what a sacrifice it is. You have to admit—it's an awfully long drive."

"Yes, well, let's get on with it. Time to stop a serial killer and whatnot."

"You drive," said Doyle.

"I thought as much."

* * *

A few hours later, Doyle put down the crossword puzzle he'd been working on and asked William, who was shifting uncomfortably in the driver's seat, "Do you really think our copycat shot Unlucky Larry?"

"Hmm," said William. "To be honest, no. I don't think so. It'd be somewhat out of character for our dear Richard Belmont. He has a pretty specific M.O., and I don't see him going outside of it. Besides, shooting Unlucky Larry in a public place would be far too risky if he had further murderous plans involving elderly, wealthy women in North Dakota."

"You've been thinking about this a lot, haven't you?"

"I'm not just a gloriously handsome bloke."

"So who did kill Larry?"

"I don't know, Doyle. I don't think we have all the pieces quite yet. We'll get there, I'm certain."

"Speaking of which," said Doyle, "what if we don't get to Edna in time? Or Amanda?"

"You really can't worry about that, Doyle. All we can do is drive ridiculously fast and hope something slows down our killer. That'd be our best case scenario."

"Oh!" said Doyle.

"What is it?"

"That word. 'Scenario.' It's the answer to one of these crossword clues." Doyle picked his pen back up and filled in some squares.

"You always know how to stay focused," said William.

35

The Friendly Companion wasn't sure if the lack of sleep was getting to him, or if he was becoming paranoid. He'd passed several squad cars on I-94. Too many. But he was careful—he never drove more than two miles under the posted speed limit. He simply couldn't risk being pulled over. The possibility of the bitch in the trunk making a ruckus was too great. Then that could lead to bloodshed. Typically he had no problem with that, as long as it wasn't his own.

A car behind him was making him nervous. It wasn't a squad, but the driver of the car kept pulling up beside him and looking at him. Why? Did he know something? Or was he just mesmerized by the bloody and inflamed flesh of his face? God, that bitch—as sexy as she was—had unfortunately figured out his weakness. It wasn't exactly a pickle allergy. He had strong allergic reactions to vinegar. Always had. He figured it out in grade school when doing the classic vinegar and baking soda volcano trick. His teacher thought he was play-acting as though the sudsy solution felt like actual lava. Then when she saw the flesh of his hands nearly melting off . . .

The person in the car was most definitely looking at him. The Friendly Companion considered pulling his gun out of the glove box, rolling down his window, and shooting the nosy neighbor right in the noggin. But that might bring even more attention that he realistically wanted at this point. After all, he had to finish the plan.

The Friendly Companion gave the curious driver a courteous wave. Then he took the next exit. The other car didn't follow.

He decided he'd need to lay low for a few hours. Maybe even take a nap. There were too many cops on the road. He had no idea if the pimple-faced kid at the gas station had called the cops, and if he had, what had he told them?

A few hours off the road. Couldn't hurt, right? Then he'd do what needed to be done.

36

manda lost track of everything. She was in the darkness of the trunk for an excruciatingly long time. She knew she had little oxygen left. If any oxygen was making its way from outside the car or from the cabin of the car into the trunk, it wasn't enough. Her breaths had becoming, short, rapid, and strained. To make matters worse, the bullet wound in her ankle was agonizing. She didn't know how much blood she'd lost. The perpetual silence made her wonder if the maniac had abandoned the car and left her for dead.

Then she heard a knocking sound. Then voices. A commotion. Then a gun shot.

Please let him be dead, she thought to herself.

Then she heard his voice though the metal of the trunk. "Don't do anything stupid, or I'll shoot you in the head. Understand?"

She didn't have enough energy or air to respond.

The trunk opened. Sweet, delicious air rush into her lungs.

"Get out," said the killer. He grabbed her by the wrists and yanked her out of the trunk. Amanda limped along as he dragged her to a police squad parked right next to the vehicle they'd been in. She was so confused by the presence of the police car, she'd almost missed the body of the cop laying on the ground between the two vehicles.

"Get in the back seat." He shoved her towards the squad car.

The fact that she wouldn't be in the trunk was a blessing, but she wasn't so naïve as to think things would be getting better for her.

He pushed her into the backseat of the squad and flung the door shut. She watched out the window as he removed the shirt and hat from the cop on the ground. Amanda looked away when she saw the trickle of blood flowing from the policeman's head.

The killer walked around to the driver's side of the squad, opened the door, then climbed in. He affixed the cop's hat on his head, and pulled the cop's button-down over his own sweaty and slightly bloody white dress shirt.

"What a great day," he said. "I got to take a little nap. We got a new vehicle to use. And look—he left us a full tank of gas!"

"Great," said Amanda.

The killer turned around and faced her. He glared at her through the mesh wire that separated the backseat from the front seat.

"Let's make a rule. You say absolutely nothing from here on out, and I'll make your death quick and painless. How does that sound?"

Amanda didn't respond.

"Good." He turned forward, reached a hand down to his trousers and scratched his crotch.

"Itchy?" asked Amanda.

He turned around and stared icily at her.

"Sorry," she said.

The killer put the already-running car in reverse.

"How's the face?"

"Goddamn it," said the killer. "This is going to be a fucking long car ride."

Amanda smiled.

"Don't worry. I promise I won't talk the entire time. Just most of the time."

The killer grunted, turned the squad towards the freeway, and hit the accelerator.

"Did you know you'll be spending the rest of your life in prison? That'll be a long time to think about all the horrible things you've done. Of course, you probably get off on that. That is, if you haven't torn off your own hoody-hoo from scratching so much."

"This car has a trunk," said the killer.

Amanda didn't respond.

"That's what I thought. Don't worry—this won't be much longer."

37

Doyle, please turn off that horrible station," said William. "I don't like any of this music. And what exactly is a 'Dierks Bentley' anyway? Is that some sort of vehicle?"

"He's a country singer," said Doyle. "But I agree, let's change the station. I'm not a big country fan, either."

Doyle turned the knob, trying to find a station that didn't have a lot of twangy guitar. Finally, he let it rest on a local news station.

"... *policeman from Kidder County was found shot to death behind the Dew Drop Motel. All resources are being utilized to find suspects in this case. If anyone has any knowledge of* ..."

"Do you think?" asked Doyle after the station went to a commercial break.

"I wouldn't be surprised," said William. "It's probably our guy."

"The radio person said 'policeman' right? As in, not a policewoman? As in, not Amanda?"

"I believe that's right, Doyle. Yes."

Doyle breathed a sigh of relief. "Okay, so how far are we from Kidder County?"

"We're going through it right now," said William. "Although we don't know how long ago this murder took place. He could be light years ahead of us."

"Drive faster?"

"If you insist." William put the pedal to the metal.

"Whoa, not that fast," said Doyle. "Let's not get pulled over by every cop on the way to Garrison."

"I'm pretty sure they're otherwise occupied with finding the cop-killer. Wouldn't you agree?"

Doyle nodded. "Actually, that makes sense. Okay. Go as fast as this thing can take us."

"That's my plan," said William.

38

dna Myrtle rocked back and forth on her rocker. *Rock. Rock. Rock.* It'd been a rather pleasant day so far. The wind was a little chilly, but nothing she couldn't handle. She mostly stayed inside anyway. She didn't like to miss her programs. Especially *Jeopardy*. She didn't always know the answers . . . err, questions, rather. But that Alex Trebek was one handsome fella. Even without the moustache.

She was quite surprised when Tommy Doogan had stopped by the house this morning. She supposed he didn't like being called Tommy anymore; probably Tom or Thomas. But to Edna, he'd always be the little boy who grew up across the street. He was always a good boy. It's no wonder he became a police officer.

Tommy'd had a worried look on his face. He'd said someone called him and said a psychopath was headed to Garrison. To see her. She laughed. Why of all places did the crazies show up at Edna's doorstep?

Edna had sent Tommy on his way. She said she wasn't scared, and, truth be told, she wasn't. She'd been to this rodeo before. Even the scariest of men could be taken down with something as simple as a rolling pin. Although she wouldn't plan on *that* little trick working every time.

Edna continued to rock. It was almost time for the Final Jeopardy round. Trebek was about to give the category when she heard a vehicle roll up in her driveway.

"Oh, dear," she said to herself. Slowly, she lifted herself out of the rocker. She made her way to the door. She pulled away the curtain to see a police car sitting the driveway. It wasn't Tommy's car. Her eyesight wasn't great, but she could tell it wasn't a Garrison squad. Actually, since Tommy drove the only cop car in Garrison, it was pretty easy to use a little logic to figure out that whoever was in her driveway was not from around here.

She could see someone in the backseat of the car. A woman? Didn't see that too often. At least, not in Edna's small, virtually crime-free town.

The policeman made his way to her door. His face was red. Scarred. He looked like something out of a horror movie.

He'd noticed that she was watching out of the window. "Good afternoon, ma'am! Mind if I speak with you for a moment?"

Edna reached to the side of her door. Right underneath a framed photograph of her deceased husband was one of her favorite possessions. Something she'd had near her for the past twenty-five years. Ol' reliable.

Edna Myrtle lifted the shotgun. It was heavier than she remembered, but she still aimed it just fine. She pulled the trigger, letting loose an explosion that sent her a couple feet backwards, but she still stood on her two feet.

Her ears rung something terrible, but she walked back to what used to be a glass door. She was pleased to see the supposed policeman scramble back to the vehicle, clutching his bleeding arm.

That worked even better than the rolling pin, Edna thought.

She lifted the shotgun again and aimed at the car. She let loose another blast. Now she wouldn't hear a dang thing for days, but she was actually having fun. She looked out just as the car pulled away. That last potshot took out a headlight.

Psychopath, my foot, Edna thought. *More like wuss of the year.*

She yanked out a drawer in a nearby armoire and pulled out a couple shells and reloaded the shotgun. Just in case.

With loaded gun in hand, she sat back down in her rocker. She noticed the local news was on. *Dang it, I don't know who won Jeopardy*, thought Edna. *This was quickly turning into a lousy day.*

Maybe she'd treat herself to a little ice cream later. After all, she deserved a reward for her efforts.

Okay, chocolate sauce, too.

39

The Friendly Companion jammed the gear shift into reverse and stepped on the gas. "Change of plans," he said.

"Looks like that stings." Amanda smiled.

"Shut up," he said, attempting to drive while simultaneously trying to inspect his arm wound. "That old bitch was packing heat."

"Obviously. Maybe you shouldn't underestimate people."

"Maybe you should stop talking before I put a bullet between those pretty eyes of yours."

Amanda didn't respond. The Friendly Companion took that a sign that she was scared. That was good. That meant his ability to instill fear in his victims hadn't been completely stolen by that old bitch. Maybe he'd made a mistake by sticking so closely to Dillman's original plans.

Amanda asked, "Why are you doing this?"

"It's in my nature."

"No, I mean the whole copycat thing. It seems weak. It's like you want to be a big scary monster, but you don't have the strength or creativity to be your *own* big scary monster. You had to rip off someone else's idea."

He stared at her in the rear-view mirror. He didn't like that she was talking. Not only was it disobeying his orders and disrespecting him, but it was also distracting. He kept driving down Main Street, looping around Ye Olde Apothecary, driving past Wally the Walleye, then turning back onto Main Street.

"It's not just about me," said the Friendly Companion. "It's the idea. After me, someone else will pick up the torch. It's about being part of something incredible. You'd never understand."

"Well, it seems a little short sighted. Most copycats are just that— copycats. They lack confidence, so they take on someone else's guise. Besides, don't act like you're copying the Zodiac. You're copying a pickle murderer. Not only is the concept ridiculous, but only one person would be stupid enough to try to emulate it."

She stared back at his face in the rear-view mirror with great ferocity. The Friendly Companion didn't like it.

"You're playing with fire, little girl."

"It doesn't matter," said Amanda. "You're going to kill me anyway. So I might as well go out letting you know what an idiot you've been. Where exactly does this brilliant plan take you? Do you think you'll get away? The old lady knew you were coming. It'll only be a matter of time before the authorities have you in handcuffs."

"Not gonna happen," he said. He wouldn't let it happen. It's true, he probably couldn't follow his original plan at this point. His chances of making it to Canada were unlikely if the police were on his trail. Even if he made it, he would no longer be able to blend in. The blondie took care of that with the little scene she caused in the convenience store. His face still ached horribly. He had plenty of money he'd deposited under a false identity at various international banks, but that no longer mattered. Not that his exploits were ever about the money.

If it came down to it, and he couldn't escape, then he'd go down in a blaze of bloody glory.

* * *

Amanda didn't like the desperation her captor was exuding. She'd been intentionally pushing him, hoping she could keep him unfocused. If he grew confused or distracted, that's when he'd likely make a mistake she could exploit. But desperation was not good. That's when bad things happen. He could decide that Amanda was no longer worth the trouble of having around.

He kept driving around the block in circles. Why? Either he was deciding what he was going to do next, or he was literally and figuratively in a spiral. He could be looking at ending things. If that was the case, she'd have to change tactics, and fast.

Deciding a new tack would be prudent right about now. "Listen, I know I'm giving you a hard time. Obviously you kidnapped me for a reason. Either you wanted to use me for ransom, or you had other plans."

"I had other plans," said the Friendly Companion, scratching his crotch and wincing in pain. "Those plans have changed."

"Ransom is a terrific idea, though," said Amanda. "It may be your best chance to get out of this mess. You can even claim it was your idea."

"Nope."

Amanda swallowed hard. "Are you sure?"

He nodded and looked at her in the rear view mirror. He adjusted the mirror downward, so the only thing she could see in the reflection was his horrible red puffy face smiling at her.

* * *

In a moment of clarity, it came to him. It was so obvious. He'd only passed the dang thing about ten times.

He parked in the small lot next to the fishing museum, grabbed his gun off the passenger seat, and stepped outside the car. He opened the rear driver's side door and said, "Get out. Don't bother screaming. That'll just end with a bullet in your brain."

Blondie looked scared again. That restored his confidence. He looked up at the giant fish statue. A tiny ladder ran up the backside, probably for maintenance. But it was high up—far higher than a person could access by jumping. He needed a rope. Or something.

The Friendly Companion grabbed the girl by the collar and pulled her towards the small brick building. She was limping from the gunshot wound he'd given her.

He opened the wood door and a bell echoed through the small space. An old man sat on a stool in a corner behind a desk covered in brochures. He wore a fishing hat covered in dozens of tiny colorful lures. "What can I do for ya?" Then he saw the gun held to Amanda's head. "What in God's name—"

"Do you have a rope I can use?" asked the Friendly Companion. "My girlfriend here really wants to ride the fish."

"Oh, you can't ride the fish." The fisherman's eyes were as wide as the Walleye's. "That's way too high up. You'd break your melon if you fell off." His eyes never left the gun.

"We're not too concerned about the fall."

The old man scratched his head. "I don't have a rope, but I have a ladder."

Amanda groaned.

The Friendly Companion laughed. If there was one thing he learned from his travels was that old fashioned folk like this museum curator could never tell a lie, even if someone's life was on the line.

The old fisherman moved slowly, but he made his way to the back room and dragged out a standard step ladder.

"Want me to set it up for you?"

"That'd be great," said the Friendly Companion. "My hands are a little full."

"That's no way to treat a lady."

"Keep your mouth shut and set up the ladder."

The weather-beaten old salt grumbled, but set up the ladder as told. "Be careful now. I don't want to see anyone get hurt."

"Of course. Now go back into your museum or whatever it is. We'd like to have some private time."

"Okie dokie." The old man hesitated before going into the building. He was staring at Amanda.

The Friendly Companion pointed his gun at the curator. He took the hint and went back into the fishing museum.

Pointing the gun back at Amanda, the Friendly Companion said, "Climb."

"Why?"

"Because I said so."

"No."

"Either go up, or you can get a bullet in the head. Your choice."

She paused, then conceded. She climbed up the step ladder, then leapt from the step ladder onto the small maintenance ladder on the backside of the fish.

"How high do you want me to go?"

"All the way," he said. "Get to the top."

"Why?"

"It doesn't matter."

"If you're going to kill me on top of a ridiculous, oversized fish, I'd like to know if there's any meaning behind it."

He knew she was just trying to buy time, but he didn't think there'd be much harm in throwing her a bone.

"Mae Sanderson tried to kill herself by jumping off this fish," he said. "It didn't work. She was in so much pain. The man she loved and trusted ended up being a sadistic serial killer. Her family turned against her. Everything she had was gone. The irony was that Fred Dillman was in exactly the same position. Sitting all alone in a prison cell. No friends. No family. He also wanted to kill himself."

Blondie was three-quarters of the way up. He could see that she was shaking. He wondered if she was that scared, or if the chilly wind was making her shiver. He also noticed the bottom of her jeans were red with blood. She was probably getting weak from blood loss.

"How do you know he wanted to kill himself?" she asked.

"I was there," he said, smiling. "I was just a kid then. My dad was a warden. He was so excited to bring me to his prison. Just for a day here or there. He wanted me to know how important he was. I didn't know anything about Fred Dillman. To me, he was just a strange man who wanted my candy bar. So I gave it to him. I had no idea he was a severe diabetic. It killed him. I killed him. I didn't mean to."

"That's why," said Amanda. "You're not just a copycat. You feel responsible."

"Something like that. My dad couldn't stop talking about it. He brought it up all the time. How I'd killed a man. I think he was proud of me. It was probably something he wanted to do, but never had the guts."

"Do you really think he'd want you killing all those good, innocent people?"

"My dad died from autoerotic asphyxiation. I really don't think it matters what he thought."

"You've had a pretty messed up life," said Amanda.

"Thanks for understanding," he said. "Now jump."

"What?"

The Friendly Companion smiled. He raised the gun. His finger stiffened against the trigger.

* * *

Doyle thought they'd be doing Edna Myrtle a favor by showing up at her house and warning her of a serial killer that could potentially be on his way to see her. The shotgun blast to the side-view mirror of William's car suggested that Ms. Myrtle was not exactly grateful. Or trusting.

"Let's get out of here," said Doyle. William reversed in a hurry and sped around the block towards Main Street.

"I'm disappointed," said William. "I thought we were on to something. That house was the logical place for Richard Belmont to go next. I'm shocked he didn't."

"Maybe he did," said Doyle. "Maybe that's why Edna Myrtle was all aflutter. They could have come here and left already."

"Right," said William.

"Hey, it's possible. I'm just saying—"

"No, you're right. Look there."

At first Doyle didn't see anything. Except for the ginormous fish statue. That was pretty hard to miss. Then he saw something move. He realized what he thought was a fin was actually a person. He could only see her from the backside, but the long blonde hair looked familiar. Then he saw the man standing on the ground, pointing a gun at her.

"That's Amanda," said Doyle. "That's *my* Amanda."

"Okay, let's be very quiet," said William. "I'll try to sneak up behind—"

"Fuck that," said Doyle. "Get ready to hop the curb."

"No, no, we're not going to—"

Doyle unbuckled, leaned over and lifted his leg and stomped his foot down on top of William's. The car lurched forward and bounced in the air as it hit the cement curb. Doyle and William smacked the ground with a thud, grass and dirt flying behind them as the wheels tore up the neatly sodded lawn near the fishing museum.

The car surged forward. Doyle saw fear on the disfigured man's face. Fear of imminent danger. The man pointed the gun directly at Doyle and got a shot off just as the car plowed into him, pinning him against the fish statue.

The gun flew from the man's hand. He screamed.

Doyle looked at William, surprised to see a bullet hole in the headrest right next to him.

"That was close," said Doyle.

"Great plan," said William sardonically.

Doyle heard a shrill scream. He leapt out of the crumpled, smoking car to see Amanda hanging by one hand from one of Wally the Walleye's fins.

Standing underneath her, Doyle yelled, "Let go! It's okay!"

"It's too far!" yelled Amanda.

William came up behind Doyle. "It really is too far. That would be another really bad plan."

"Just drop, honey. It's okay. I'm here for you."

"You're going to break something," yelled Amanda.

"No, I won't. I've come all this way to rescue. Just let go!"

Amanda let go. She fell on top of Doyle, slamming into him and knocking him to the ground.

Doyle heard something crunch. Then felt horrible, horrible pain.

"Oh, ow," he said. "Ouch. Get off. Get off."

"Doyle, there's a ladder right here," said William. "That would have been far safer and more efficient."

"I think you broke my shoulder," said Doyle. "Or maybe my arm."

"Sorry, Doyle," said Amanda. She leaned down and kissed him.

* * *

It was all coming to an end. His brilliant plans. His deliciously fun encounters in homes throughout the midwest. His role as the Friendly Companion was now done.

He could no longer feel anything in the lower half of his body. On the up side, the dreadful itchiness had finally disappeared.

He saw the gun on the ground a few feet away. He'd dropped it. How stupid was that. Although, in his defense, he was *hit by a fucking car*.

His arms still worked. He wasn't completely paralyzed. If he could just lean to the side. Even just a little bit, then maybe he could . . .

* * *

"I can't believe you found me," said Amanda.

"It was kind of a lucky guess," said Doyle.

"I don't care. You did it. I love you."

Just as Amanda was about to lay another lip lock on Doyle, a deafening blast echoed though the air.

Doyle couldn't hear anything. He didn't feel any additional pain except for the sore shoulder and arm, so that was a good thing.

Amanda was fine. She was on top of him, although she was frantically looking around to see what had happened.

Doyle couldn't see William, and that sent a chill up his spine. He felt a hand on his back, and he turned to see William, who crouched down beside him. William nodded at him, then pointed at the car. The disfigured man was still there, but he was slumped to the side with a red hole in the center his maroon puffy face.

"Where—?" Doyle opened his mouth to ask where the shot came from. Was it self-inflicted? Did William shoot Amanda's kidnapper? Doyle felt a quick pang of jealousy that he hadn't been the one to pull the trigger.

Then Mae Sanderson stepped out from behind a bush next to the fishing museum. Doyle watched her lips move, but he couldn't make out what she was saying.

"Hold on," he told Amanda. He rolled out from beneath her, wincing in pain. He ran up to Mae. Her eyes were wide and she was shaking.

Doyle held out his hand. "Give me the gun."

She looked at him. "That was him, right? The copycat?"

"Yes, it was," said Doyle. "He's gone now."

Mae Sanderson nodded, then handed the gun to Doyle, who bit his lip from the pain in his arm.

"I'm sorry," she said. "Freddy destroyed my life. This world doesn't need any copies of him. The original was bad enough."

"I understand," said Doyle.

William lifted Amanda to her feet, who bit her lip from the pain in her ankle. William held her up as they walked over.

"What happens now?" asked Mae.

"I'll call the police," said William. "They'll take our statements. I have a feeling, based on the circumstances, you're unlikely to face any charges."

"It doesn't matter," said Mae. "I've been living in my own prison for decades."

"Maybe it's time you let that go," said Amanda. "You did a good job. You saved us."

Mae Sanderson smiled. "Thank you."

"Go ahead and call the police, William," said Doyle. "The faster we get home, the better."

"I'll second that," said Amanda. "This is a lovely town, but our visit wasn't exactly a vacation."

PART IV

Two Weeks Later

Minneapolis, Minnesota

"There's no place like home when you're not feeling well."
-Garrison Keillor

40

oyle sat in front of the glowing computer screen in his office. Although it was the middle of the afternoon, Doyle had the shades drawn. The sunlight hurt his eyes, especially with the painkillers he was taking. He inadvertently reached for his bottle of Honey Weiss with his injured cast-clad arm, sending a searing bolt of pain through his body. Technically he wasn't supposed to have any alcohol with the pills, but Doyle assumed that something with the word "honey" in its name couldn't possibly cause any harm.

William was in his own office, which doubled as his bedroom. Doyle could hear him snoring. This was nothing unusual; William slept odd hours. He was still recovering from the North Dakota trip. After all, William didn't sleep a wink the entire weekend. Doyle had taken naps here and there, but William worked right on through.

Doyle checked his e-mail again. Still nothing new. He was hoping for some kind of case to come his way. He was out of prospects, money was drying up, and he still owed Hanratty cash for joining him on the North Dakota investigation. He considered calling Amanda to see if she could get out of work early. Maybe she'd be up for an exciting, yet affordable date.

Doyle grabbed the bottle of beer with his good arm, took a swig, set down the bottle, then took out his cell phone. He was about to dial Amanda's number when he heard a knock on the building's front door.

He ran through his mind who might be there to see him. Hanratty? No—he'd be at the Martiniapolis this time in the afternoon. Amanda? She was scheduled to work through the evening. A potential client? Boy, he hoped so.

He stood, walked to the door, and opened it to find himself staring at a familiar face. It wasn't a friend, per se. But definitely not an enemy. He was too stunned for words.

"Are you one of the gentlemen on the sign?" The man at the door was wearing a suit, a red necktie, and to Doyle's surprise, a pair of red sneakers.

"Yeah," said Doyle, gathering himself. "I mean, yes. I'm Detective Doyle Malloy. You can call me Doyle."

"I'm Garrison Keillor. Feel free to call me Garrison Keillor. Or Garrison. Or Mr. Keillor. I'm not particular."

"I know," said Doyle. "I mean, I know you're Garrison Keillor. What are you doing here?"

"You're a detective, correct? This is a detective business? As it so happens, I have a situation that requires some detecting," said Garrison.

"Absolutely," said Doyle. "Sorry to leave you on the doorstep. Please, come in."

"Thank you."

As Garrison Keillor entered Doyle's place of business, Doyle felt ashamed and embarrassed by the untidiness of the place. Hopefully Mr. Keillor would overlook the random pop cans, beer bottles, and candy bar wrappers that permeated the lobby.

"This looks like my father's old fish house on Leach Lake," said Garrison.

"Don't get me wrong," said Doyle, "we get a lot of work done here. But we do like a comfortable environment. No hole in the floor, though."

"What happened to your arm?" asked Garrison, eyeing the cast on Doyle's arm.

Doyle considered the best way to explain what had happened in North Dakota.

"Giant fish," said Doyle. "Things got a little out of control."

"Tried to reel in the big one? That's dedication. I certainly appreciate that."

Doyle offered Garrison Keillor a chair and removed a Salted Nut Roll wrapper just before Garrison sat down.

"What can I do for you?" asked Doyle.

Garrison cleared his throat. "I'm not sure if you've heard, but one of the stars of my program was shot and killed a couple weeks back. I'm afraid the police have not been able to apprehend the person responsible."

"I'm well aware. I was at your show that night. And frankly, I've been trying to find out myself."

"Have you had any luck?"

"Yes and no. We thought that a man by the name of Richard Belmont was responsible for Unlucky Larry's death. He was copycat killer who took on the persona of the Friendly Companion, who robbed and killed several elderly women back in the eighties. Richard Belmont was loosely connected to Larry Sanderson. He was married to Unlucky Larry's daughter Clara. As it so happens, one of Larry's other daughters, Mae, had dated and fed information to the original Friendly Companion."

"Well, that must be it, then," said Garrison.

"Not necessarily," said Doyle. "Richard Belmont was a vicious, sadistic killer of elderly women. But it was always at their homes. That was his M.O. Shooting someone in a public place would have been highly unusual. Not to mention that he had very specific plans of who he was intending to kill. Taking out Larry that night could have easily derailed his plans, and I don't think he would've taken that risk."

"It sounds like this Richard Belmont was just as dedicated to his plans as you were to that giant fish."

"Richard Belmont used to be dedicated. Now he's just dead."

"That's quite an awful pun," said Garrison.

"I realized that as I was saying it. I'd actually like to take that one back."

"Let's move past it."

"Sure," said Doyle.

Garrison Keillor folded his arms. "So who do you think killed Larry?"

"I think it's somehow tied into the Friendly Companion case. I'm just not sure how. Or who."

"Do you mind if I ask who hired you? Or are you investigating out of your own curiosity?"

"Frankly, it's out of my own nosiness. Business has not been great, so I've had some free time on my hands. I had the privilege of stopping a serial killer, so I can scratch that one off the 'ol bucket list. But the fact that I haven't pinpointed Larry's killer still really bothers me. I'll continue researching and putting the clues together, but so far I'm going in circles."

"That reminds me of my cousin who was born with two left feet," said Garrison. "But that's digressing from the issue at hand. The reason I came here was to hire you to solve Unlucky Larry's murder, since it seems the police have had very little luck, no pun intended. However, I suppose it would be rather pointless since you're already working on it."

Doyle shrugged his shoulders, then winced. "I have to stop doing that."

"I can see you've been through a lot," said Garrison. "Tell you what. I came here prepared to hire you. If you can find out who did this to Larry and bring him, or her, to justice, I can give you ten-thousand dollars."

"That's awfully generous, Mr. Keillor, but I can't . . ."

"It's not just me. I certainly don't mean to give that impression," said Garrison. "The entire staff of the show has pooled their money together. We all want to see justice. Please—will you consider it?"

"Of course, I'll try. How can I say no to that? But I'm at a bit of a loss. I've been through this many times."

"Maybe you should take a step back," said Garrison. "It's like when you lose your car keys. If you search everywhere, you'll never find them. But if you think about it for a while, consider all the places you'd been and the things you'd done, perhaps retrace your steps, then you find them where you never would have looked otherwise."

Doyle nodded. "Retrace my steps. I can do that."

"Although this isn't just like finding your car keys. Generally speaking, car keys won't attempt to kill you if they discover you're hot on their trail."

"That's comforting," said Doyle. "But you're also right. Thank you for this, Mr. Keillor. I'll do everything I can."

"I'm glad to hear it," said Keillor. "Now I must be off. I'm performing a rousing rendition of Lady Gaga's 'Poker Face' at next week's show. We'll be using an accordion and mandolin. It should be quite breathtaking."

"That sounds like something I may want to go see," said Doyle. "But then again, I may be busy."

"I'm sure you will be," said Keillor. "Good luck."

* * *

"William," said Doyle, knocking on the door to William's room. "Hey, William. You up?"

William groaned loud enough to be heard through the door. Doyle caught the words "go away" and "sleep."

"William, guess who was here! Garrison Keillor."

Doyle heard frantic activity from within. The door opened. William had red eyes and a terrible case of bed head. "Who keeled over?" he croaked.

"No, no one keeled over. I said 'Garrison Keillor.' He was here."

"Oh. I see. So—no one is dead?"

"Not today. But it's early afternoon, so there's still plenty of time."

"I'm quite tired," said William.

"I see that. Did you sleep at all last night?"

"No, I'm afraid not. I was going through my notes on Larry Sanderson. I also did some Internet research and performed rudimentary background checks on people who'd worked with Larry or gone to college with him—essentially all of his Facebook friends."

"Any luck?"

"No, it was a big waste of time. And then I fell asleep."

"Well, at least you tried," said Doyle.

"What brought Garrison Keillor to our office? He's the showman, right?"

"Yes, he actually came here to hire us. To find Larry's killer."

"Interesting," said William. "So you're saying we may actually have an opportunity to make some money."

"That's exactly what I'm saying."

"What are we waiting for? We should get to work," said William. "We need to devise a plan. Let's brainstorm. I'd like us to develop a sophisticated outline of Larry's life, the people he'd been in contact with, giving special focus to the year leading up to his death. Then if we can cross-reference with the—"

"I'm going to the bar," said Doyle.

"Excuse me?"

"Garrison Keillor told me to retrace my steps. That way, I might stumble on the clue we've missed."

"You're going to get intoxicated with your chum Hanratty."

"No, no. Don't be ridiculous. I might have a beer. But I'll also solve the case."

"Sure, Doyle. Just remember that this has become substantially more important now that we have money on the line."

"Oh, believe me. I fully understand. We have plenty of bills that need paying. We'll work it out somehow. No need to fret."

William grimaced.

"You should shave, William. You're looking awfully . . . rugged."

"I'll take a shower," said William, with a heavy sigh.

The Martiniapolis Tavern was fairly dead, although that was typical for a Monday afternoon. A few construction workers were eating an early lunch at one of the tables. Other than them, Hanratty was the only other patron. He was sitting at the bar drinking a Grain Belt Nordeast.

Doyle slapped his old friend on the back. "How are those legs, buddy?"

"I was able to get here. That's good enough. How's your arm?"

"I keep forgetting it's broken, so I try to do things I shouldn't with it. It hurts pretty bad."

"You'll figure it out. If not, the cast will come off eventually."

"Not anytime soon, the way it's been going. I've tried to open doorknobs, but instead I ram the cast right into the door."

"That's not smart," said Hanratty.

"I realize that."

The bartender approached Doyle. It wasn't the usual bartender. This kid couldn't be much older than twenty-one. His face was full of piercings, and he had tattoos that reached up from under his shirt and seemed to strangle his neck.

"What can I get ya?" the kid said.

"The usual," said Doyle.

"I'm not the regular bartender, so I have no idea what your usual is, mister," said the kid.

"Blueberry daiquiri," said Doyle.

"You're kiddin' me."

"Nope. I'm dead serious. And make sure it's frozen. If I don't hear that blender whirring, I'm going to be very upset."

The kid raised his eyebrows, shook his head, and walked away. Presumably to make Doyle's delicious beverage.

"What brings you here?" asked Hanratty.

"I came here based on the advice of someone you may know."

"Who?"

"Garrison Keillor."

"Really?" asked Hanratty. "He likes the Martiniapolis?"

"Well, not exactly. I mean, he didn't say that. He just told me to retrace my steps. Make sure I didn't miss anything. He wants me to find out who killed Unlucky Larry."

"You've been working on that since it happened. Does Garrison Keillor know he might be barking up the wrong tree?"

"I'm the right tree," said Doyle. "I just have to put things together, that's all."

"Sure."

The young bartender brought the blue beverage and set it in front of Doyle.

"No umbrella?" asked Doyle.

"I don't think we have those," said the kid.

"The usual guy gives me an umbrella. What's his name? Terry, right?"

"Yeah, Terry Johansen. He's been out for a couple weeks."

"Vacation?" asked Doyle.

"Not exactly. Bereavement."

"Oh, I'm sorry to hear that."

"Yeah, his mom died," said the kid. "You know that guy on the news? The Friendly killer guy? He got her."

"Really?" said Doyle. He exchanged glances with Hanratty. "How long ago?"

"'Bout three or four weeks ago, I guess."

"I thought you said he was on bereavement for a couple weeks."

"He worked for a few days afterward. You know, to make sure the place was in decent shape before he took off."

"Where did he go?"

"The funeral, I think. He's probably still with his family there. They're out in . . . oh, where is it? It's the place that sounds like a donut. Bismarck?"

"When did he leave?"

"Hmm." The kid scratched what he was trying to pass off as chin whiskers. "I'm trying to remember. It was pretty sudden. It was on the weekend, which is a pretty bad time to leave. We don't exactly have a huge staff here. And I remember because it was the day after that guy was shot. The Prairie Home guy."

"This is starting to seem like more than a coincidence," said Hanratty.

"I agree," said Doyle.

The young bartender looked confused. "What are you guys talking about?"

Doyle paused to take a drink. "Do you know if he went to the *Prairie Home Companion* show, by any chance?"

The bartender shrugged. "Yeah, I know he went. He bought my tickets."

Hanratty leaned over the bar. "*You* had tickets to *Prairie Home Companion*?"

"So? I used to listen to it with my grandparents. They raised me. Is that a crime?"

"Of course not," said Doyle. "Isn't it strange that he wanted to go just a few days after his mom was killed?"

"Not really," said the kid. "I just figured he needed to blow off some steam."

Hanratty whispered to Doyle, "Terry was here the day after Larry was shot. He must have heard us talking about it, panicked, then fled."

"Why would Terry kill Larry?"

Hanratty whispered back, "He must have thought Larry was responsible for his mom's death."

"Maybe," whispered Doyle. "Or maybe it was revenge. What if he did the same research that William and I did, figured out that the Friendly Companion had killed his mom, and assumed it was Mae Sanderson. We thought it was Mae for a while, too, until we discovered Belmont was getting information from a different teller."

"Do you think he would have figured out there was a copycat killer and not told anyone?"asked William.

Doyle thought about it. "Mae thought maybe someone was sending a message when her father was killed. She thought someone was playing tricks on her."

The young bartender slammed his hands on the bar. "What the hell are you guys talking about?"

"Do you happen to have Terry's cell phone number?" asked Doyle.

"Sure," said the bartender.

"I'd like to have it, please."

"I'm not so sure that's a good idea."

"I'm a detective. I'm not asking. Give me the number."

The kid reluctantly nodded. "Okay." He took out his cell phone, scrolled through his contacts, and then rattled the number off. Doyle took out his notebook and jotted the number down.

"Thanks, kid. Now I need to ask you to not call that number. At all. And if you do, we'll know about it, because we'll be tracing it. Got it?"

"Yeah, sure. Whatever."

"Great," said Doyle. He laid a twenty-dollar bill on the bar. "Thank you for the information."

Doyle took a final drink of blueberry daiquiri, then cringed at the inevitable cold headache. "That's the stuff," he said.

oyle sat in his car outside the Martiniapolis. He tried calling Amanda on his cell phone, but she wasn't answering. This wasn't unexpected, but he was really hoping that during a lull—probably when she was working on paperwork—that she'd pick up the phone. No such luck.

He tried William. Fortunately William was typically not as busy as Amanda, and he picked up right away. "Yes, Doyle? Did you have too much beer? Need a ride?"

"Nope. Listen, I need you to do something. Find out everything you can about Terence Johansen. He's a bartender at the Martiniapolis. His mother was one of the victims. I can't remember her first name."

"Hilga Johansen," said William.

"Right. Also, and this is just a hunch, see if he's related to or is in cahoots with anyone who works at the *McLean County Independent*. I'm wondering if he was somehow responsible for the article that warned Larry of his own impending death."

"I'll look into it," said William. "Should we meet up shortly?"

"Yes," said Doyle. "Gather up all your notes, photos, articles—everything. Bring it to the Saint Paul Police Department."

"What do you have in mind, Doyle?"

"I'll let you know when you get here."

"Doyle, you're not going to do something rash and stupid, are you?"

"When have I ever—oh, never mind. Just be there. Got it?"

"Got it."

* * *

Doyle parked in the employee lot of the Saint Paul Police Department, right next to Amanda's Honda Accord. Doyle wasn't an employee, but he was dating one, so he figured that was sufficient.

William pulled into the adjacent visitor's lot. Doyle stepped out of his car and waved to William, who walked over with a five-inch thick binder.

"Is this what you've been doing late at night?" asked Doyle.

"Yes, if you must know. Why, do you think I usually do something wholly inappropriate?"

"I'd almost rather you were doing something inappropriate. This is just sad."

"Doyle, this is everything we learned the past two weeks. Not just about Larry Sanderson, but also Richard Belmont, and some history on Fred Dillman as well. This is the full story. Each of their stories, undeniably tied and tangled together. Speaking of which, you were correct about the news article. It seems that Terence Johansen's brother Keith works at the paper in Minot. I have no proof he wrote the article, but that's far too much of a connection to be coincidental."

"Agreed."

"So what are we doing here, Doyle? Are we picking up Amanda? Are we going to chase down this Terence Johansen?"

"Something like that. Maybe I should just go in."

William studied Doyle's expression.

"I suppose you'll want to bring this?" asked William, holding up the file.

"If I could," said Doyle, reaching for it.

William tugged it away. "I know you think you're being clever, but you're not that talented at deception. You want to give this to Amanda's boss. To make sure Amanda keeps her job and maybe even gets a little bump in status. Meanwhile, her boss gets to take all the credit for our hard work. I suppose we won't see a dime from Garrison Keillor, either."

Doyle shrugged. "I'm sorry, William. I have a great talent for getting the people I love into trouble. It's not often that I have an opportunity to help. This is my chance to make Amanda's life a little better. Even if it means making ours a little tougher."

Doyle reached for the file again. William held firm.

"We're partners, Doyle. We need to make these kinds of decisions together."

William let go. The file was heavier than Doyle had expected, and he instinctively reached for it with both hands.

"Owww," Doyle yelped. "I have to remember to stop doing that."

William smiled. "I thought that might happen. Listen, Doyle. I love Amanda, too. And I'd do the same thing if I were you. Just don't try to pull a fast one on me. Fair enough?"

"Fair enough," said Doyle. "Thanks, William."

"Just remember you owe me," said William. "A lot."

"I know I do."

"Good. Now go be the knight in shining armor."

* * *

"And you're absolutely positive this . . . Terence Johansen," said Chief Cynthia Reiser, reviewing the final pages of William's notes, "is the man who killed Larry Sanderson?"

"I'm positive," said Doyle. "He was at the show. We've confirmed that with one of his co-workers. He had motive. His mother was killed by Richard Belmont, the man who killed his wife, Clara Belmont, just a couple weeks ago. Terence probably saw the pickles near his mom's body and put two and two together before anyone else did. I'm also guessing it wasn't too long after that when he would've called his brother at the *McLean County Independent* to dig up information on the Friendly Companion murders. Terence incorrectly thought that Mae Sanderson was continuing the murders from years ago. Only Mae was just a pawn in Fred Dillman's plan. Richard Belmont, the copycat, didn't even use Mae to get information. He used a younger bank teller."

Reiser glanced up from the notes. "So you're saying that Terence believed he was serving up justice. Eye for an eye. He figured Mae killed his mother, so he killed her father."

"That's what I'm saying," said Doyle.

Reiser stood up from behind her desk. "Why are you bringing this to me?"

"You made your position very clear," said Doyle. "You didn't want us investigating this case. The only problem is—it's in our nature. It's what we do. It was never our intention to interfere. But we did want to prevent further unnecessary murders."

"Your escapades led to Amanda being kidnapped," said Reiser. "Has she forgiven you for that?"

"I think so," said Doyle. "Or, she's at least going through the process. It could be awhile."

"Good," said Reiser. "Let me ask you a question. Why do you think I asked you and Amanda to not interfere?"

"You didn't exactly ask us, Chief. It was more of an order."

"Granted. Still, I ask the question."

"Well," said Doyle. "I'm sure you didn't want pipsqueaks like us getting in the way. I can tell you're a very procedure-oriented person. Not to mention, once the case got solved, you'd want to be able to take the credit, right?"

Reiser folded her arms and paced the office. "You're partially right, Detective Malloy. I don't like people getting in the way. And it's not just because I'm a rigid control-freak. That's in my nature, too. But more importantly, messy investigations don't lead to convictions. An arrest is pointless if a case cannot be successfully brought to court with a win for the prosecution."

Doyle nodded. "I understand that."

"But this," said Reiser, holding up the binder that William had meticulously put together, "is not a mess. Whoever put this together, whether it be you or Amanda, did a splendid job. When I get paperwork from McNulty, it looks like a monkey used a crayon. That's not to say that I approve of your methods, and I certainly don't approve of anyone disobeying my orders. But you did very good work."

Doyle was surprised by what he was hearing. "Thanks."

"You mentioned something about taking credit. I have to let you know that I have no interest in stealing anyone's credit. My detectives put their lives on the line every day, and I'll be damned if I'd take their successes away from them."

"Sure," said Doyle.

"Why are you giving this to me?" asked Reiser.

"Well, I uhh . . ." began Doyle. "I wanted to make sure that Amanda will be okay. You have to understand, I had no intention of putting Amanda's job in jeopardy. If you want to hold anything against her, hold it against me instead. That's why I'm turning our work over to you. If it's better for you to say you got this information from your proper channels, that's fine. I just don't want anything bad to happen to Amanda."

Reiser smiled. "You're trying to protect your girlfriend."

"Something like that."

"That's very noble. But really, you don't have to worry. I saw more bravery and dedication from Amanda and Steven than I've seen with any other detectives I've worked with. As long as they report to me, they'll be just fine."

Doyle sighed. "Good. Thank you."

"What do you want to see happen next?" asked Reiser.

"Well," said Doyle. "I'd like you to keep this file. Track down Terence Johansen and bring him in."

"I'll be lighting up the boards at every police department between here and Montana. Don't worry—we'll find him."

"Good."

"What do you want for all your work?" asked Reiser. "And don't say money. We're on a public budget, so we don't have that flexibility."

"I know," said Doyle. Then an idea struck him. "Do you know Garrison Keillor?"

"He's left me a voicemail every day this past week," said Reiser. "He's anxious for us to find Larry Sanderson's killer."

"Please call him back," said Doyle. "And let him know that Doyle took care of it."

Reiser shrugged. "Okay. I can do that."

"Thank you."

"You've been involved with this from the beginning," said Reiser. "Do you want to be with when we track down Johansen and arrest him?"

Doyle thought about it. "No," he said. "I'd love to, but I can't handle another drive through that state again."

43

Doyle sipped his cup of coffee. It was a little after eight o'clock in the evening. The dinner crowd had already made their exit from Mickey's Diner, and the post-theater performance crowd had yet to arrive for some late night eggs and bacon.

It was nearly October, which in Minnesota meant that a blizzard could be right around the corner. The idea made Doyle shudder. This was the time of year when he preferred to hunker down and hibernate. Since a Minnesota winter could stretch into nine months, Doyle fully understood why he didn't accomplish very much on an annual basis.

He was drained. Wiped out. He could only imagine how Amanda felt. After all, she'd been through a lot. Much more than he. Between the kidnapping and nearly falling from a ridiculously large fish, she was due for a vacation. But, not being the vacationing type, she'd gone back to work as soon as Reiser had allowed it. Though Amanda was only a few years younger than Doyle, she had substantially more energy than he did. Boy, she was impressive.

He perked up as she entered the diner. Her limp had mostly disappeared, though there was still a trace. The doctors had done a remarkable job of removable the bullet and restoring her health. She glanced to her left, then noticed Doyle to her right. She smiled.

"Oh, it's good to see you after a horrendously long day," said Amanda.

"Busy?"

"I could give up investigating and become a full-time paperwork jockey."

"Sounds pretty glamorous," said Doyle.

Amanda shrugged. "I'll take it. I still haven't fully recovered from our little excursion. Sometimes when my hand gets tired from holding a pen and filling in boxes, I remind myself that it's a heck of a lot better than riding around in the trunk of a car."

"Good words to live by," said Doyle as he drained the last of his coffee.

"I could use some of that," said Amanda. "With some Bailey's."

"You won't find that here, but you could go crazy and use some Splenda."

Amanda stuck out her tongue.

A waitress with a pot of coffee in hand, wearing an old-fashioned white-and-pink uniform came up to their table.

"Coffee, hon?" asked the waitress, already filling up Doyle's empty cup.

"Yes, please," said Amanda. "And a huge pile of bacon. Make it a BLT. I'm starving."

"We can take care of that," said the waitress, quickly heading to the next table to take additional orders.

"I need to show you something," said Doyle. "Did you watch the news today?"

"No. I was completely buried in paperwork."

Doyle reached into his pocket and pulled out an iPhone.

"Oh, Doyle—we can't afford that right now."

"Yes, we can. It was a good day. I'll explain more, but first you need to see this."

Doyle pushed a button and a video began playing.

"Is this from today?"

"Yup," said Doyle. The video showed McNulty and Jenkins behind a podium, speaking into an unnecessarily large number of microphones.

"I can't believe Reiser would let those idiots do a news conference," said Amanda. "What were they saying—"

"Shh. Just listen."

"*—thanks to help from the public and some unanimous tips*"—Amanda rolled her eyes as McNulty spoke—"*we've apprehended the man we believe to be responsible for shooting and killing Larry Sanderson, known to the public as Unlucky Larry. The suspect, who we now have in clink*"—Jenkins visibly nudged McNulty in the side—"*er, in custody, is Terence Johansen, owner and bartender of the Martiniapolis Tavern in northeast Minneapolis. He's charged with murder in the first degree. While many assisted in the investigation, the arrest truly could not have been done without . . . us. We did a terrific job.*" McNulty looked to his partner, who gave him an approving nod.

Amanda looked at the screen curiously. "How did these morons figure out who killed Larry?"

"Those morons didn't. This moron did," said Doyle, pointing at his own chest.

"So they're taking credit for your work? Those sons of bit—"

"Whoa, whoa—don't worry about it. We came out ahead."

"How did you figure it out?"

"It just took a little inspiration from Garrison Keillor. And by inspiration, I mean a giant check, which he promptly delivered to my office shortly after this press conference was held."

"I don't follow."

"Mr. Keillor offered to pay me a bonus this morning if I could find out who murdered Larry and bring that person to justice. Well, after I did figure it out, I had a little visit with your boss."

"That's kind of crossing the line, Doyle."

"Normally I would agree, but this was a special circumstance. She's very supportive of you, Amanda—of us. I think I won her over. In fact, I know we did. She personally called Garrison Keillor to tell him what we'd been through and what we accomplished."

"Okay, that's pretty impressive."

Doyle tapped the display screen on the iPhone. "We may not have gotten full credit for the investigation. But we still got the credit that matters."

The waitress came by and plunked down a cup of coffee and a BLT with a heaping pile of bacon in front of Amanda.

"This day has really turned around," she said.

"What are you doing tonight?"

"I might stop by Steven's apartment and see him. He's still off work until he's fully healed. It shouldn't be too much longer. Do you have any plans?"

"I was thinking of meeting up with Hanratty at the Martiniapolis, but that place has left a sour taste in my mouth."

"Maybe their blueberry juice has gone bad."

"Cute. No, I might just see what William is up to. Maybe I'll buy him a White Castle. I owe him, anyway."

"Sounds good. Just don't be out too late. Later tonight, you're all mine."

"Oh, really?" asked Doyle. "Am I looking particularly handsome tonight?"

"Mmm . . . no, you look really tired. But fortunately for you, I really love you," said Amanda.

"I love you, too. Sexy woman."

Amanda laughed. "Doyle—you always know exactly the right thing to say."

Doyle smiled. "Hey," he said, pointing to the object next to Amanda's sandwich. "You gonna eat that pickle?"

ACKNOWLEDGEMENTS

In my previous books I stated that writing is a collaborate effort, which indeed it is. I couldn't get away with writing an acknowledgements page without giving due credit to Jessie Chandler, Joan Murphy Pride, and Dennis Anderson, without whom this novel would be flooded with an overabundance of violence, sex, and adverbs.

But writing is only a piece of the literary puzzle. The marketing, event organizing, and publicity are just as critical for my books to make it to the bookshelves, snuggled warmly between William Kent Krueger and Jess Lourey (two other fine Minnesota mystery writers.) Without the help of some amazing individuals who were willing to go above and beyond, Doyle Malloy's literary adventures would be eternally trapped in a box in some random warehouse, like in *Raiders of the Lost Ark*.

Thank you to the following individuals for setting up and promoting events: Michele Dooley, James Orcutt, Janet Waller, Lin Salisbury, and all the excellent store managers, community relations managers, and booksellers at Barnes & Noble stores; David Enyeart of Magers & Quinn; the excellent staff of Common Good Books in Saint Paul; Monica Campbell and Connie Kline of the Anoka County Library; Katie Simning of the Ramsey County Library; and Jill Glover of the Luck Library in Wisconsin.

As always, thank you to Seal, Corinne, and Brandon of North Star Press for the terrific job of publishing and marketing my books.

Thank you to all the readers who show up at events and listen to me speak. I apologize for any inappropriate humor. Especially if you brought kids.

Thank you to Lori Lake and Dennis Anderson for their impressive technological and design skills.

Thank you to Katie Raivala of Raivala Photography in Otsego, Minnesota. See that incredibly impressive photograph on the back cover? That's Raivala Photography. Miracle workers, I tell ya.

Thank you to the communities of the many cities throughout North Dakota and Minnesota that I reference in this book. I'm sorry I let loose a fictional serial killer in your towns.

Special thanks to Garrison Keillor, for having an exceptional sense of humor, and allowing me to poke fun at his legendary show.

Thank you to my parents, friends, and family for continuous support and enthusiasm for my writing projects.

Finally, thank you to my wife, Jaclyn, who expanded my fan base by one with the addition of our son, Devin.